Mazes For Kids Ages 4-8:
Maze Activity Book For Kids | More Than 101 Mazes.
ISBN: 9798831194142

www.samirataj.com

Welcome to the family.

THIS BOOK BELONGS TO:

SAMIRATAJ.COM

SUBMARINE

SNAIL MAZE

Quick! Get to the hospital.
AMBULANCE
500 m
HOSPITAL
HOSPITAL

DEER MAZE

WHOS LETTER HAS WHAT?
1
2
3
4

MULTI-MAZE GAME

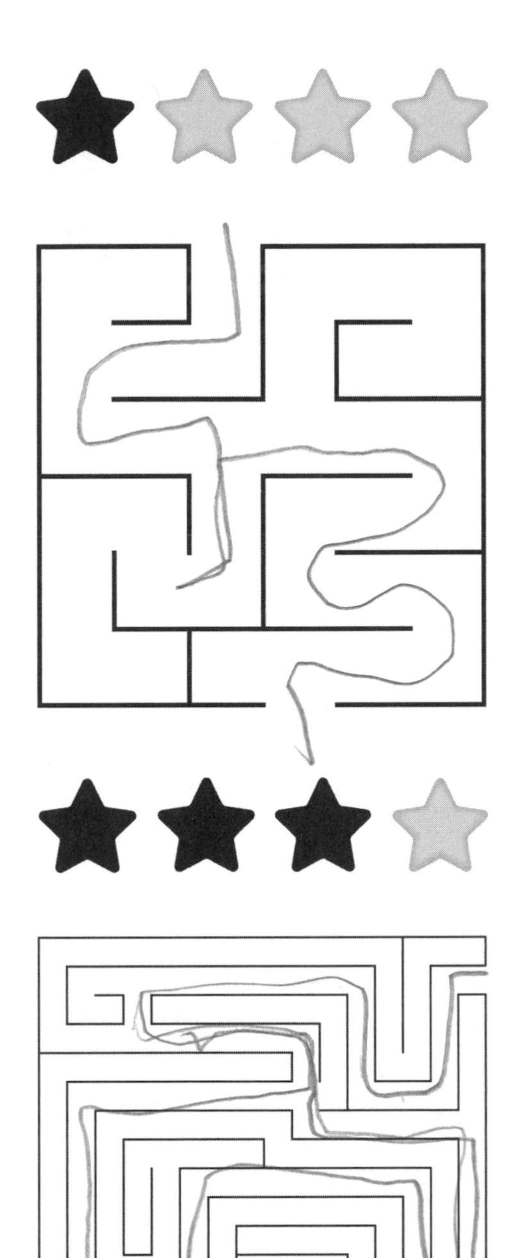

WHO'S PRESENT?

CUPID MAZE

What does SNAIL eat?

WHO WINS?

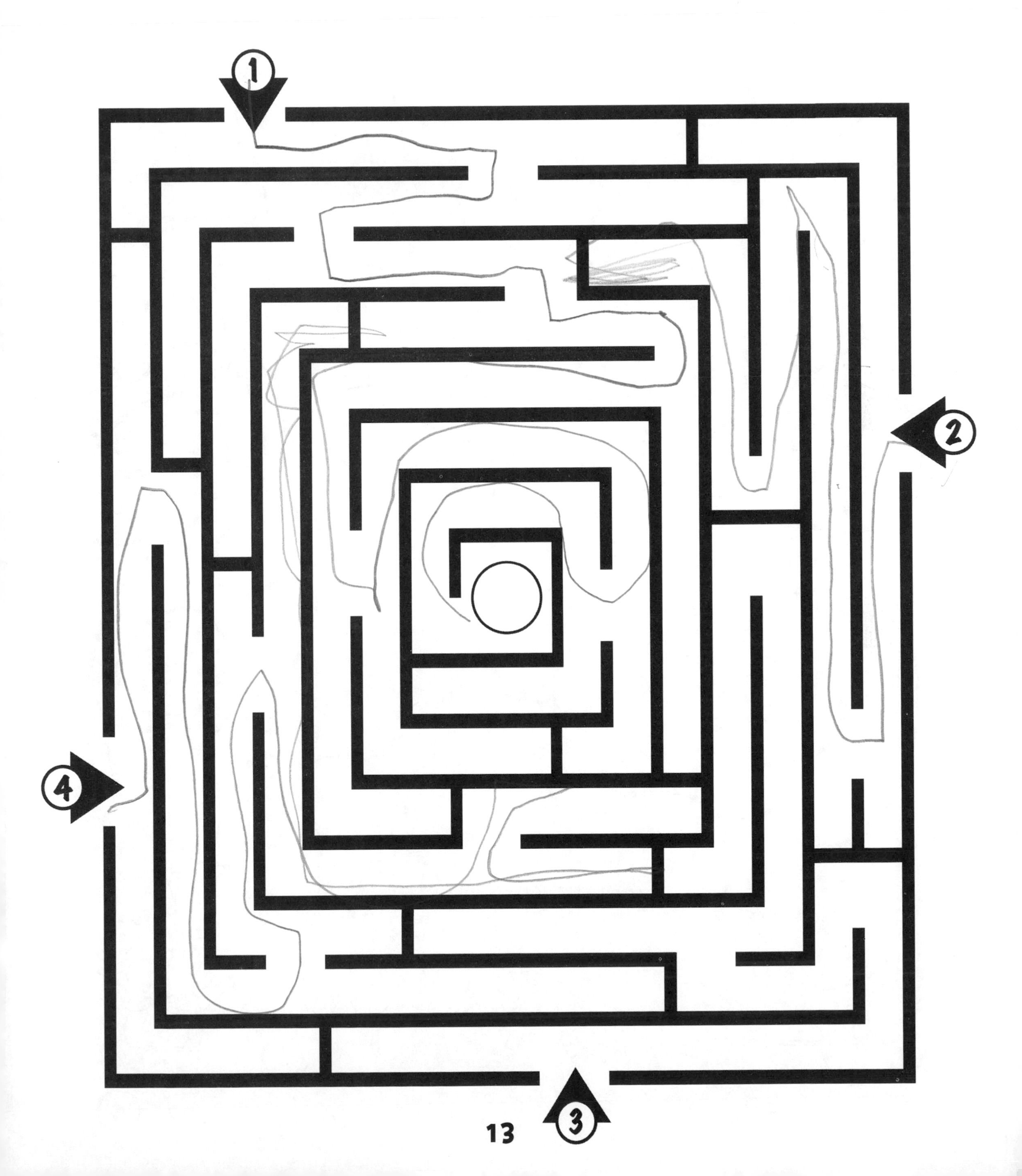

WHO'S BALLOON
1
2
3
4

SHAPE MAZE

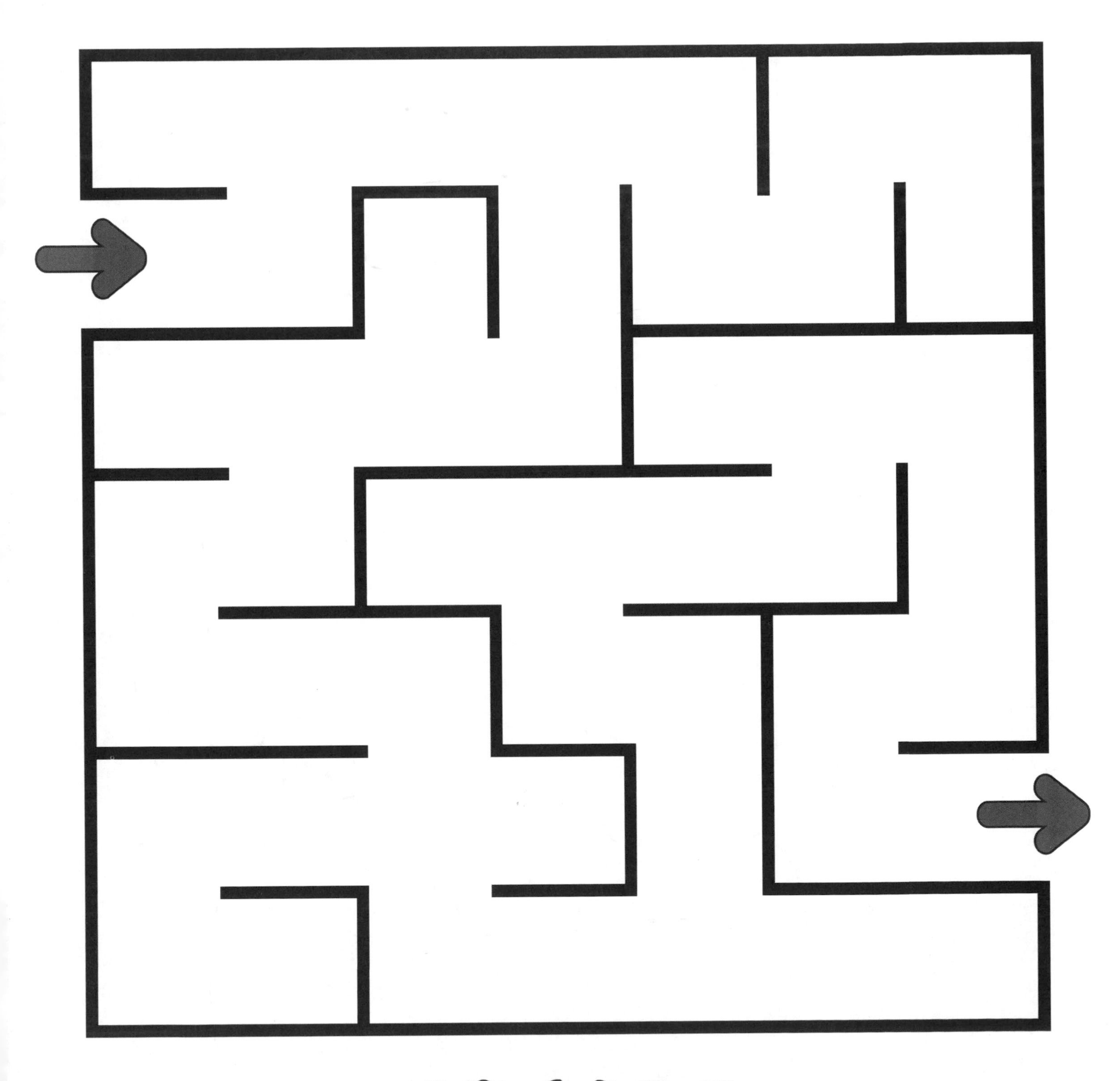

SQUARE

Bath
Time!

DOVE MAZE

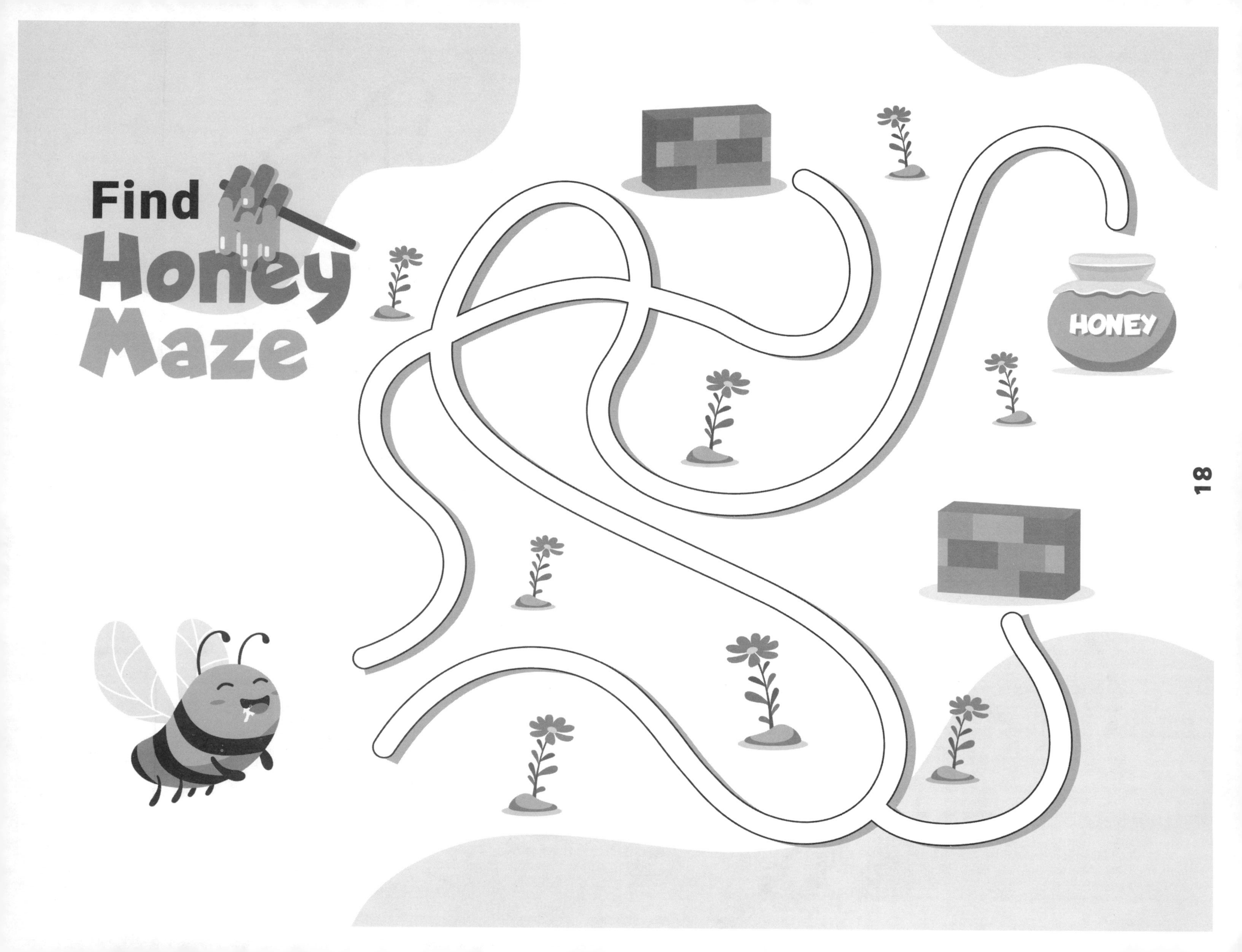
Find Honey Maze
HONEY

GORILLA MAZE

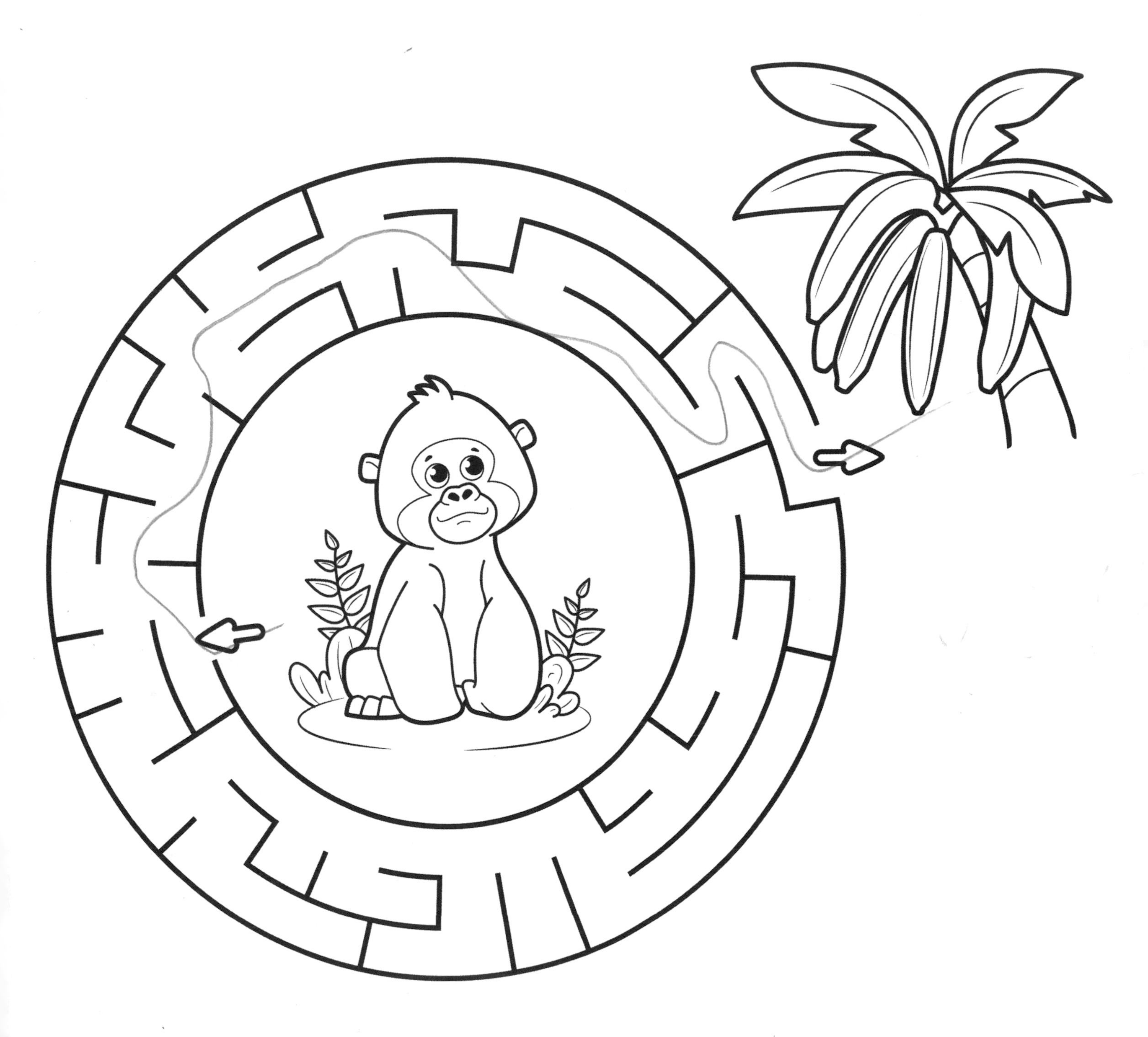

Here kitty, kitty...

WHO WINS?

LOST PUPPY MAZE

GET TO THE MIDDLE

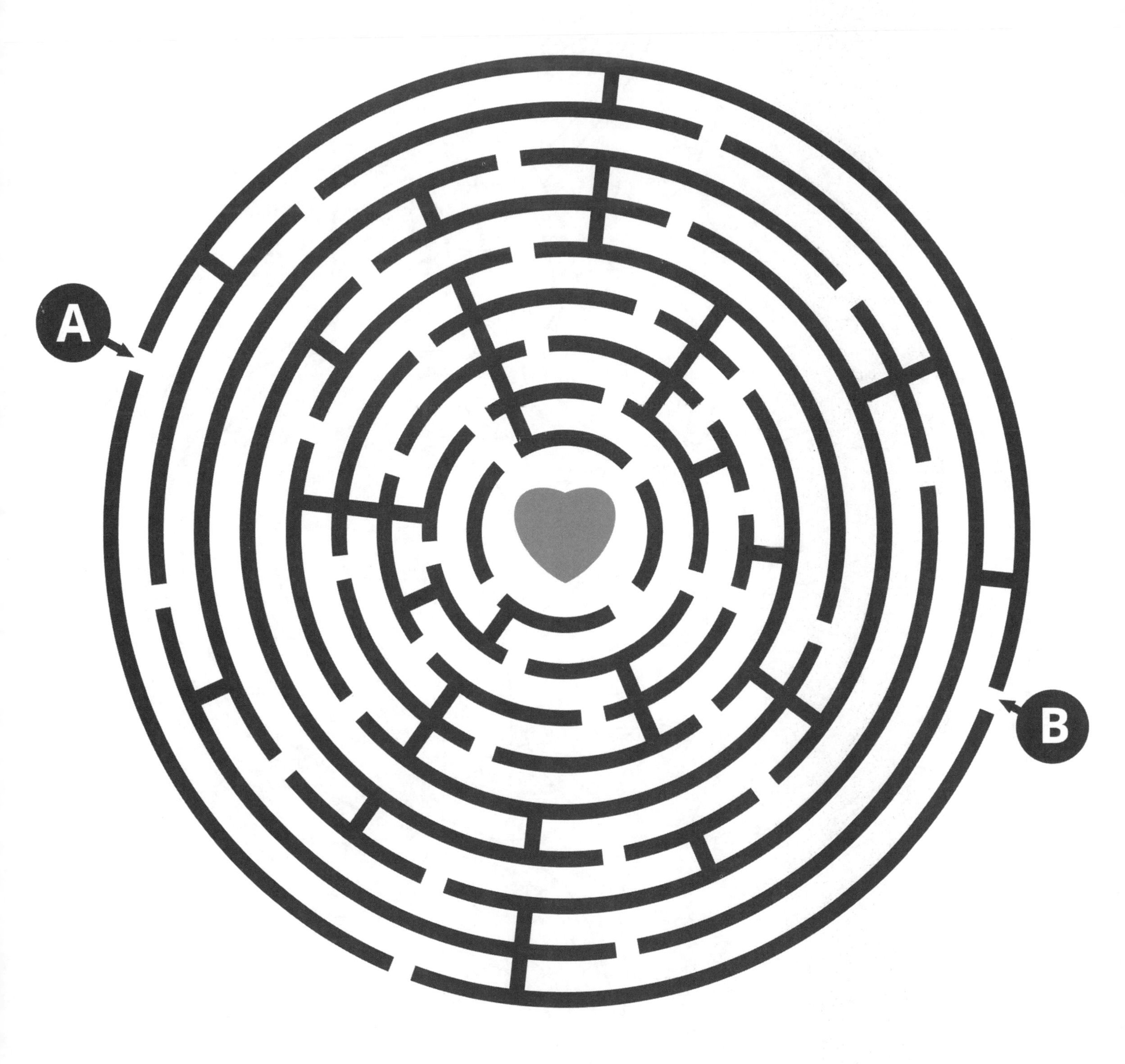

Help Mommy T-Rex find her babies.
Finish
Start

SEAL MAZE

WOLF MAZE

SEAHORSE

Here puppy, puppy . . .
1
2
3

HELP SANTA

GET YOUR GIFT

HELP BABY PENGUIN FIND THE IGLOO

RACE TO THE MIDDLE

FLYING HEART

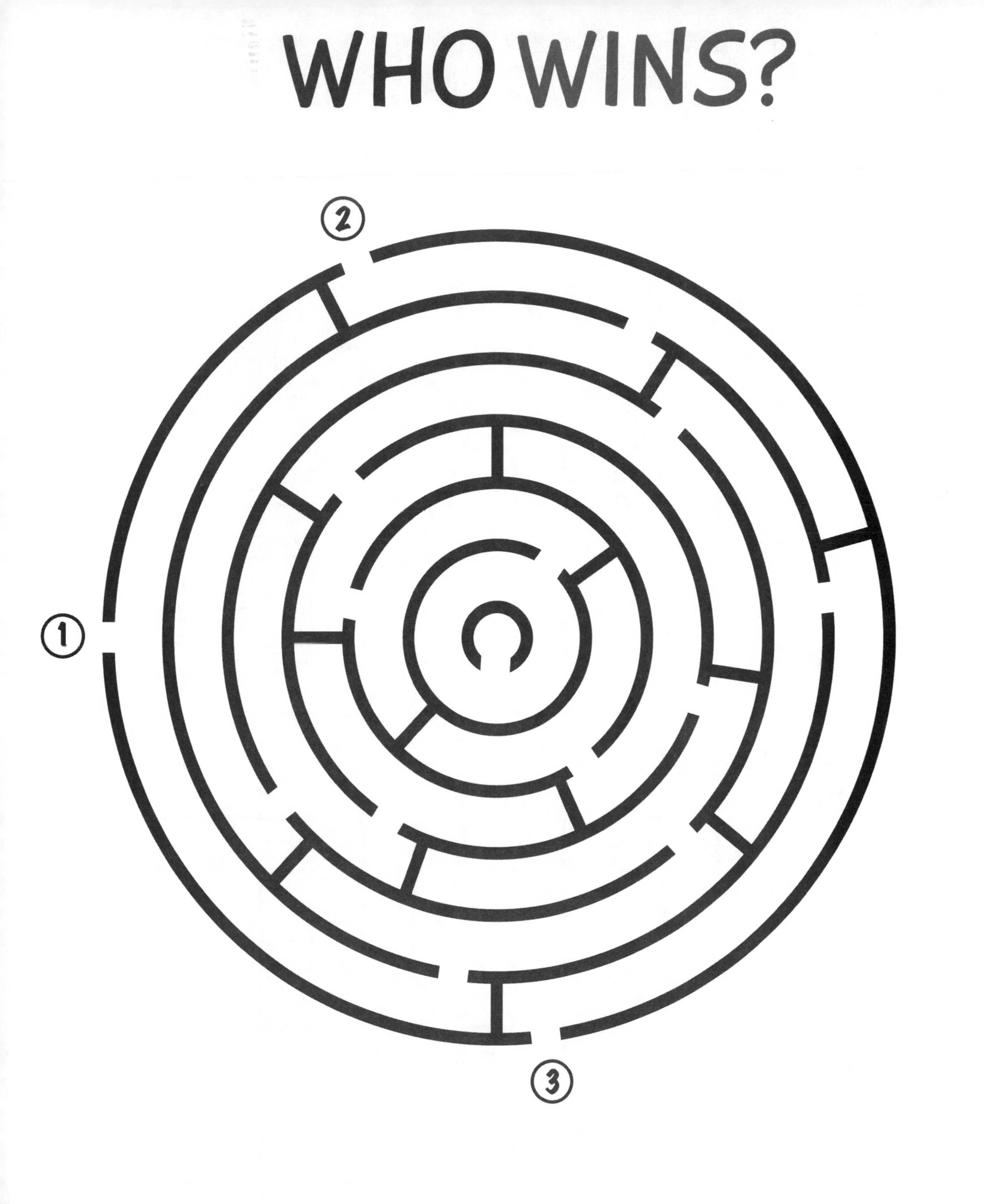
WHO WINS?
2
1
3

CAKE MAZE

Help the bunny find sweets

Cupid's Arrow hits the heart.

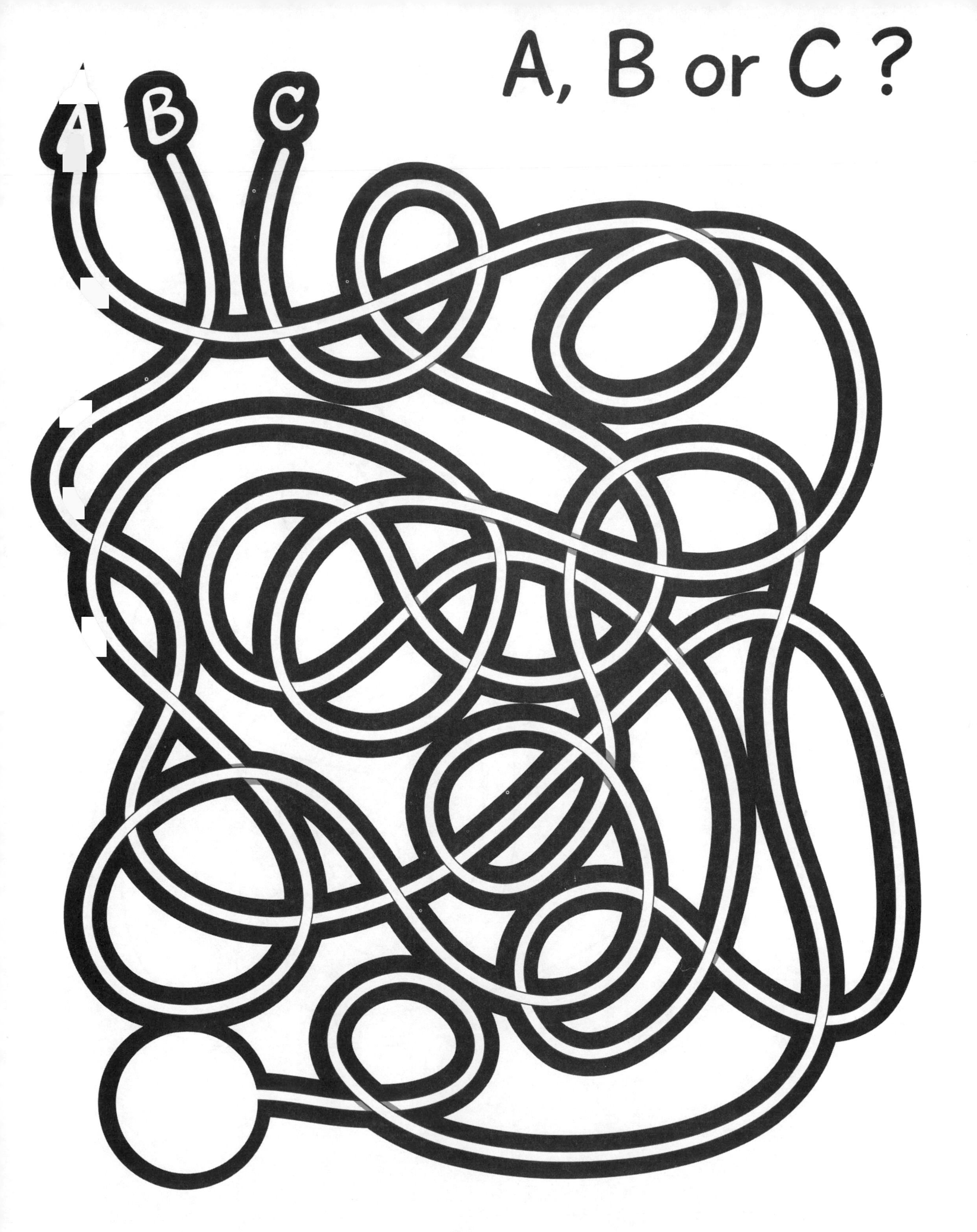
A, B or C ?
A
B
C

Which route should Bambi take?

CAKE MAZE

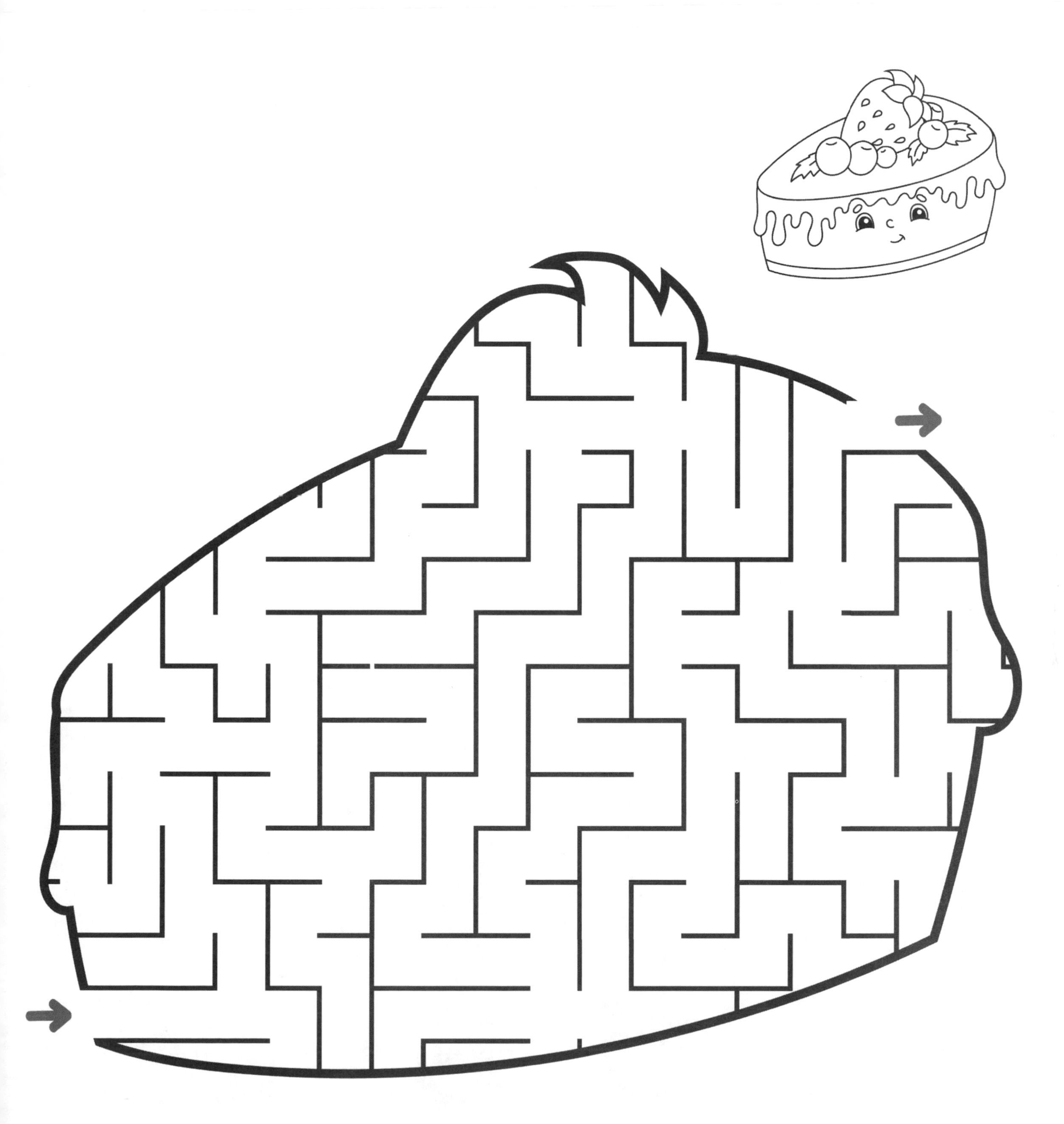

- HELP - ARNOLD TO FIND HIS BREAKFAST

WHO WINS?

Let's Find
My Baby!

SHAPE MAZE

HEART

HELICOPTER

MULTI-MAZE GAME

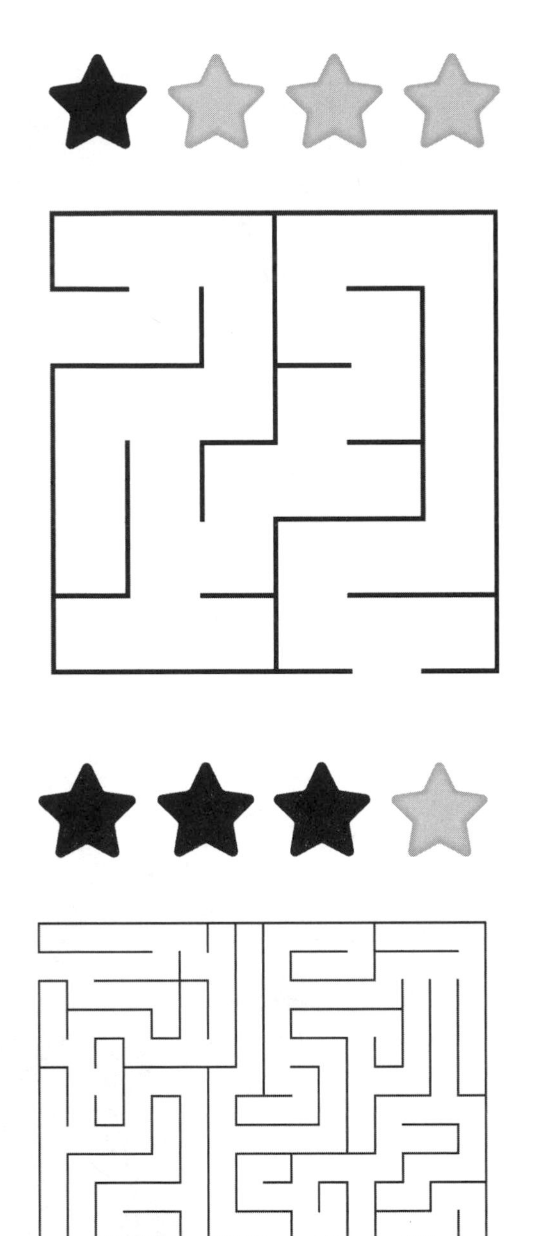

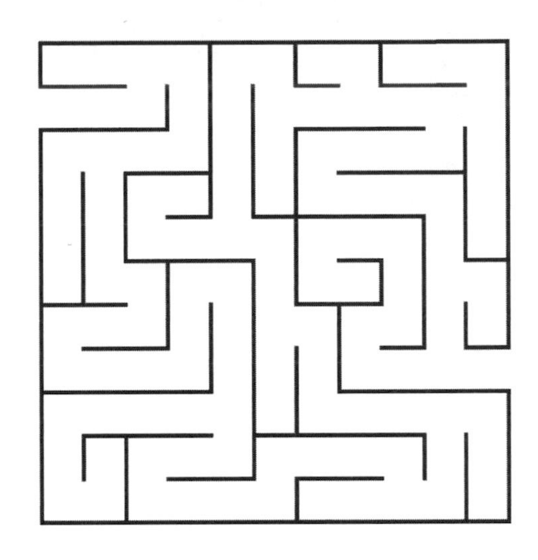

FIND MY PAW PRINT

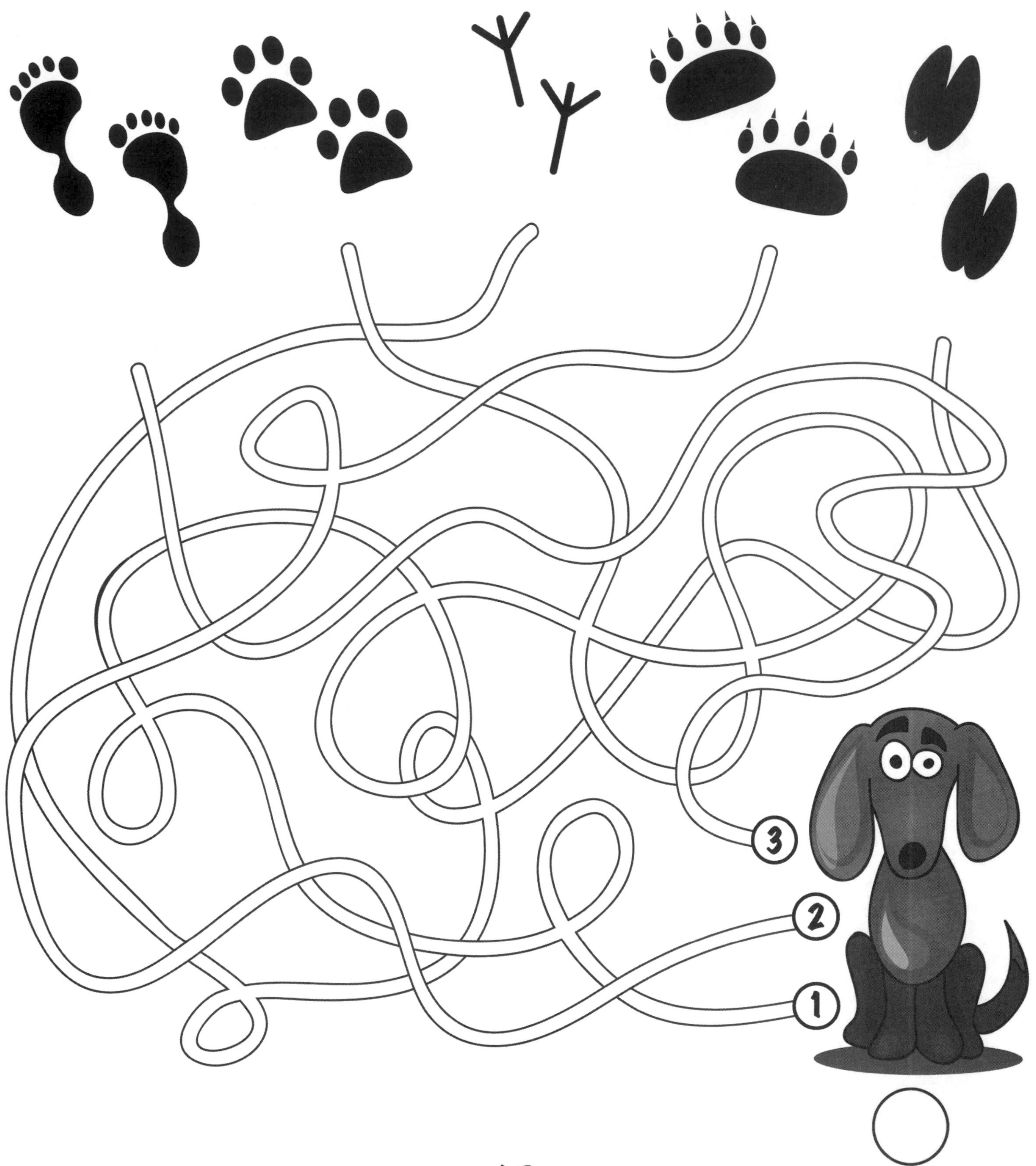

PLANT MAZE

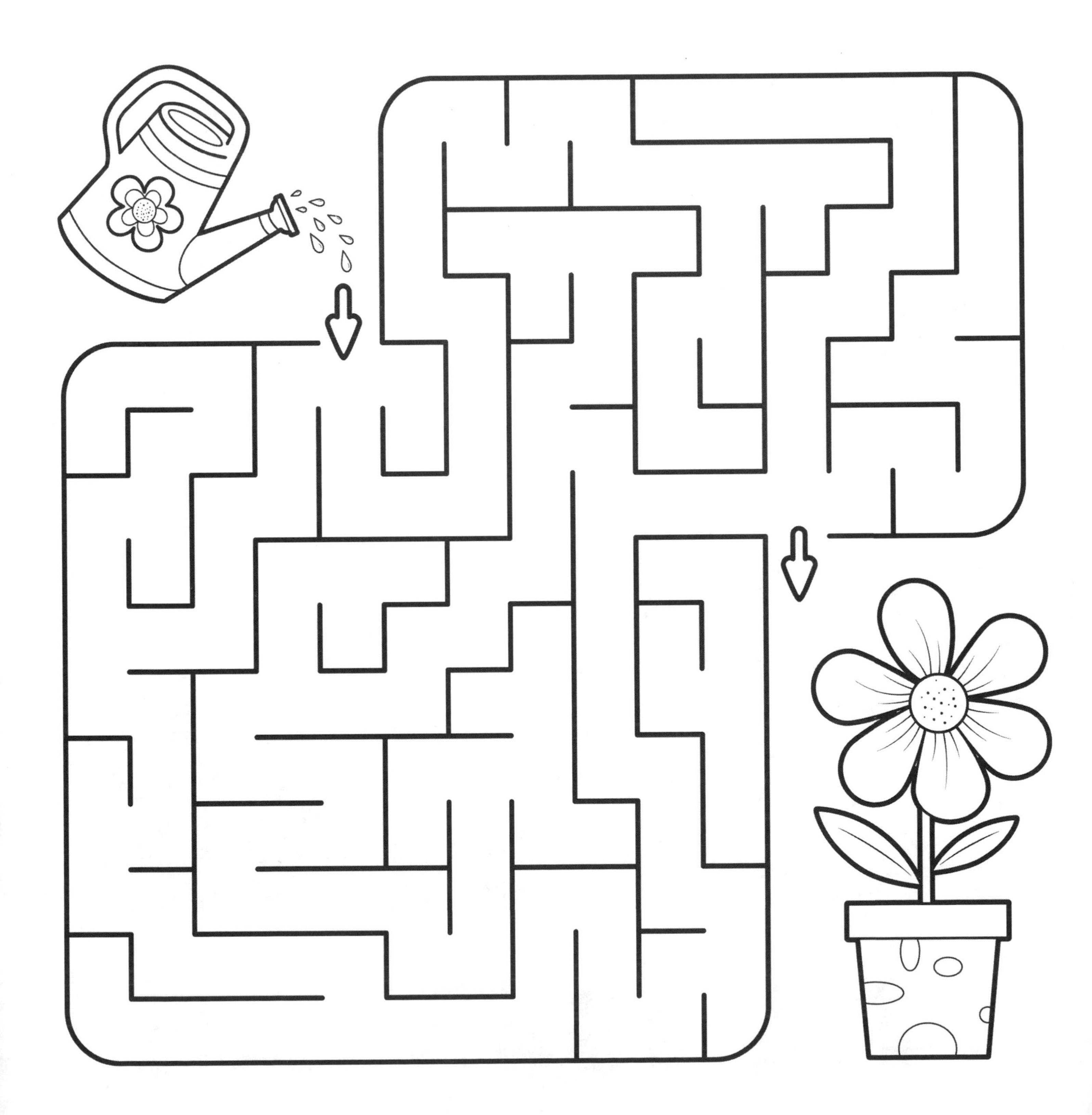

CRASH! BANG!

FIX YOUR CAR

WHICH WAY HOME?

Start
Finish

DRAGON MAZE

GREAT ESCAPE

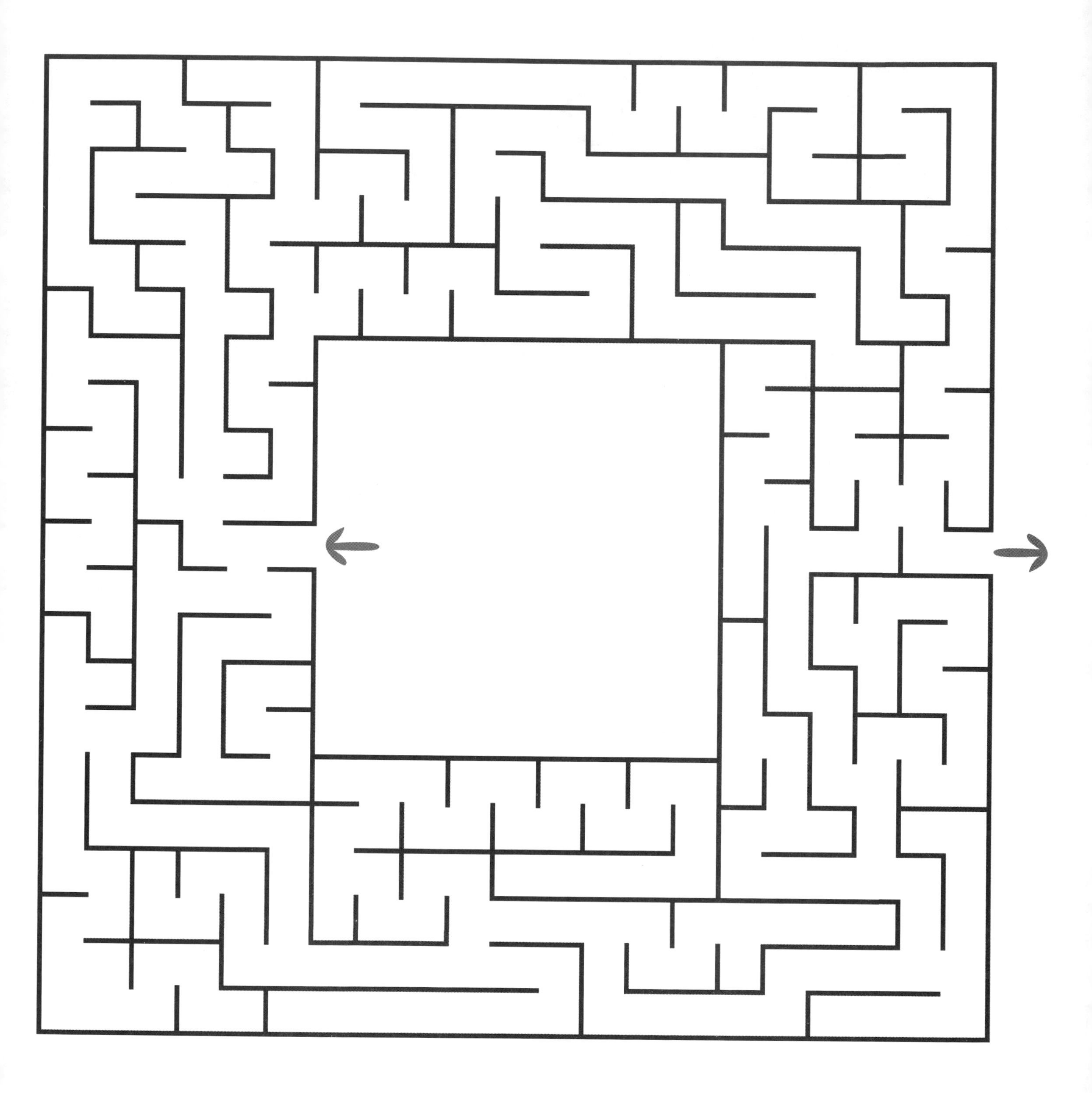

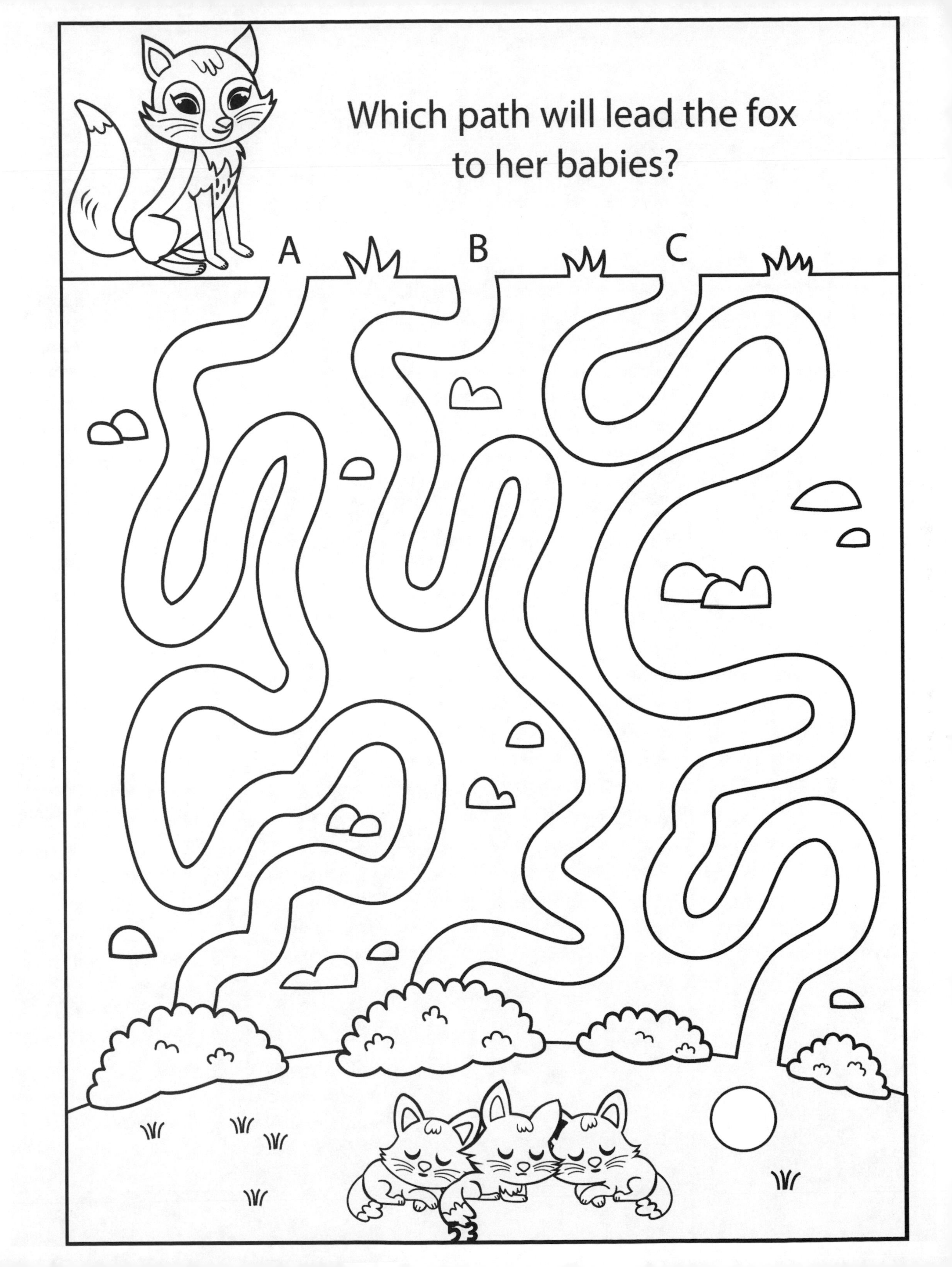
Which path will lead the fox
to her babies?
A
B
C

FIND THE POLICE
POLICE
POLICE

WHO WINS?

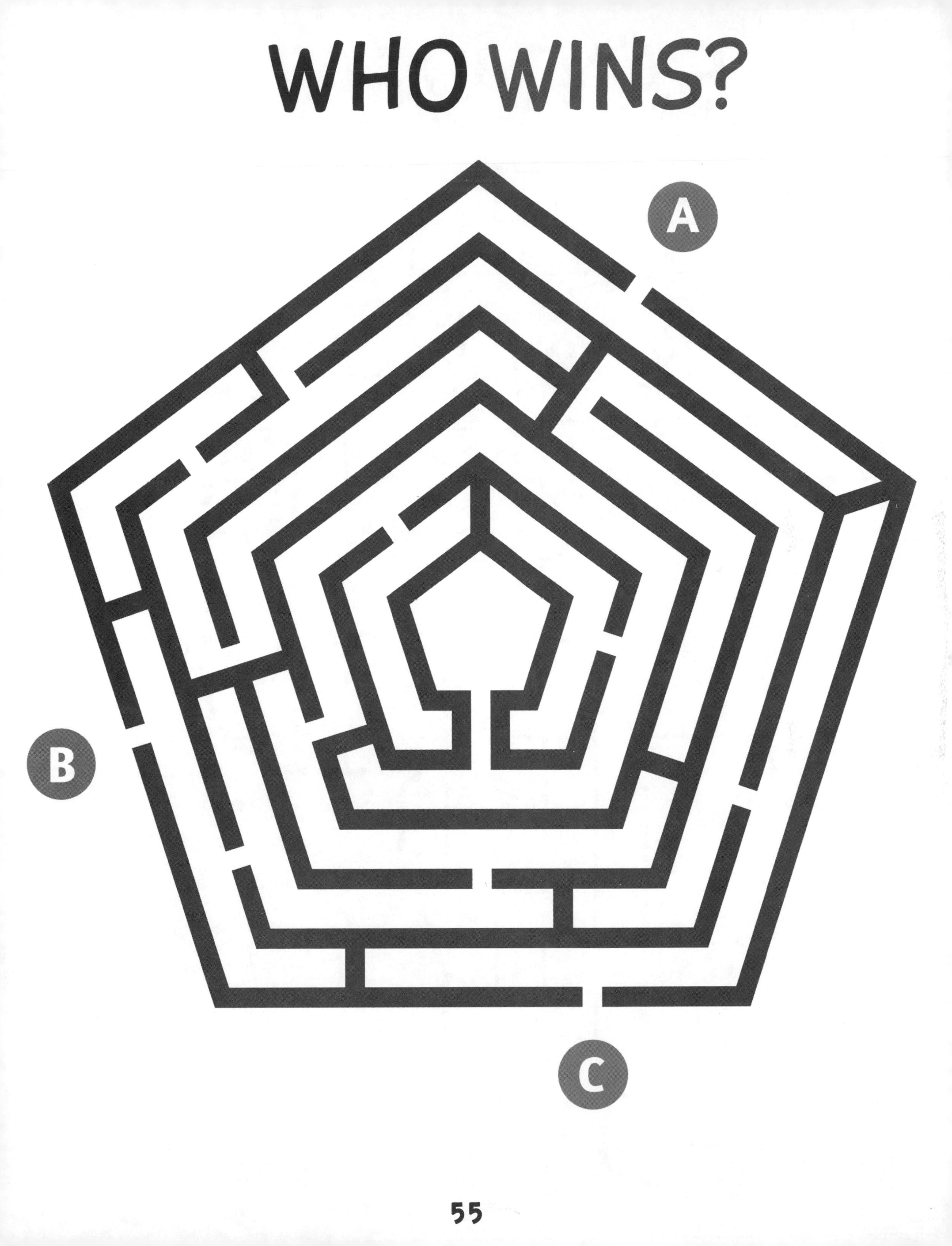

SANTA MAZE

PLANT MAZE

Treasure Hunt!
Finish
Start

3 RUN MAZE

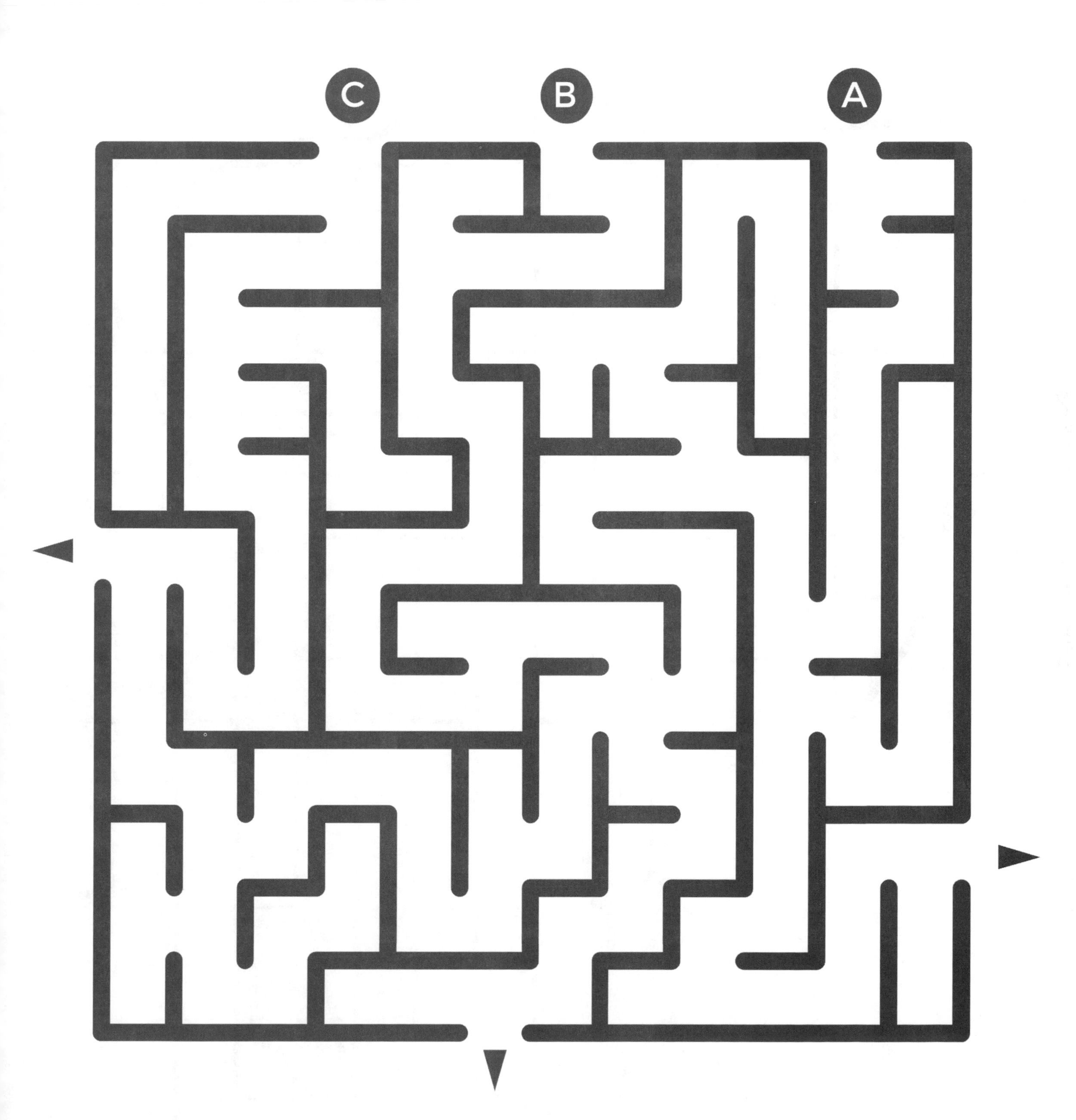

PUPPY MAZE

SAVE THE PRINCESS

design your own maze game.

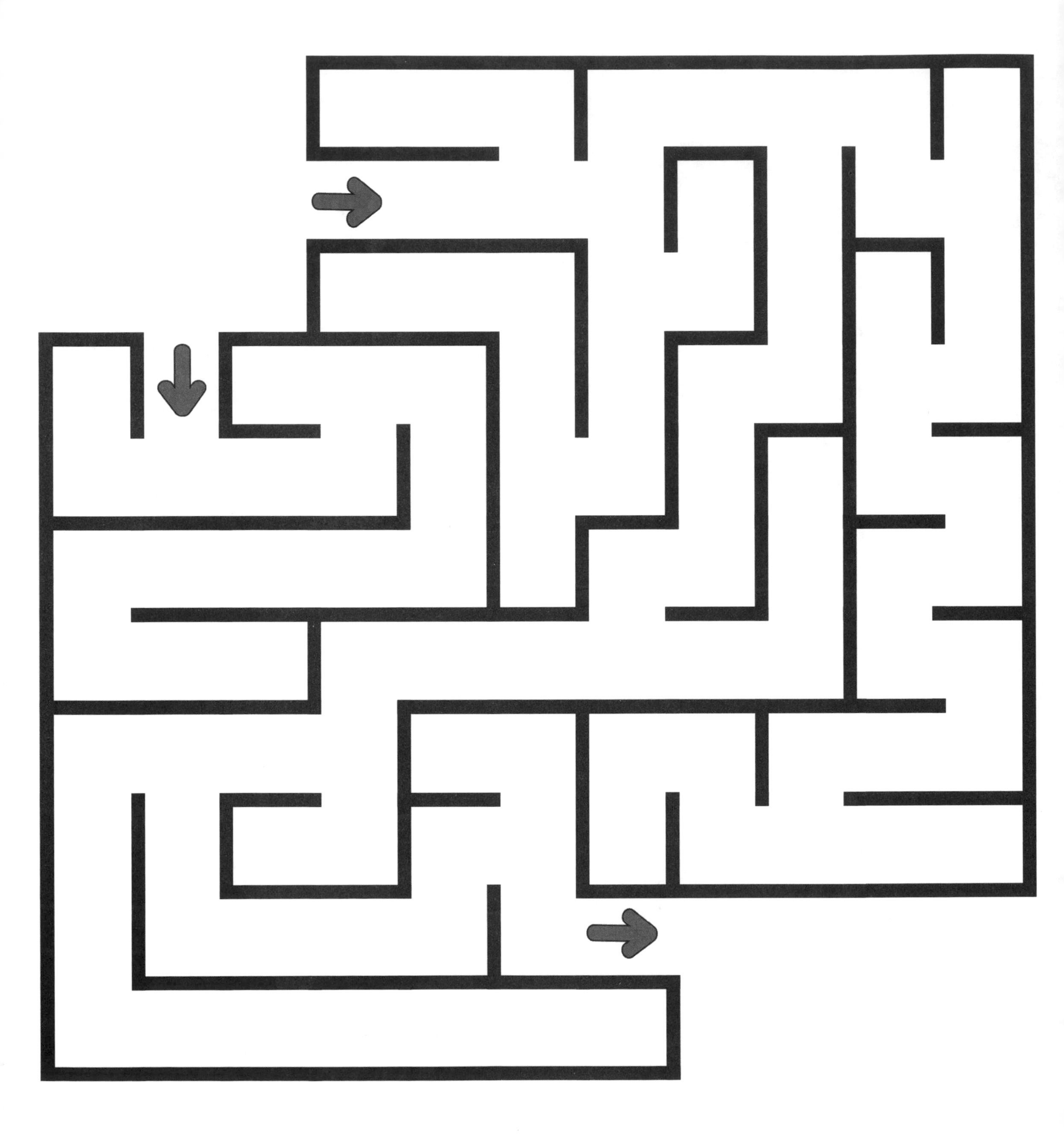

BE THANKFUL

FOR YOUR GIFT

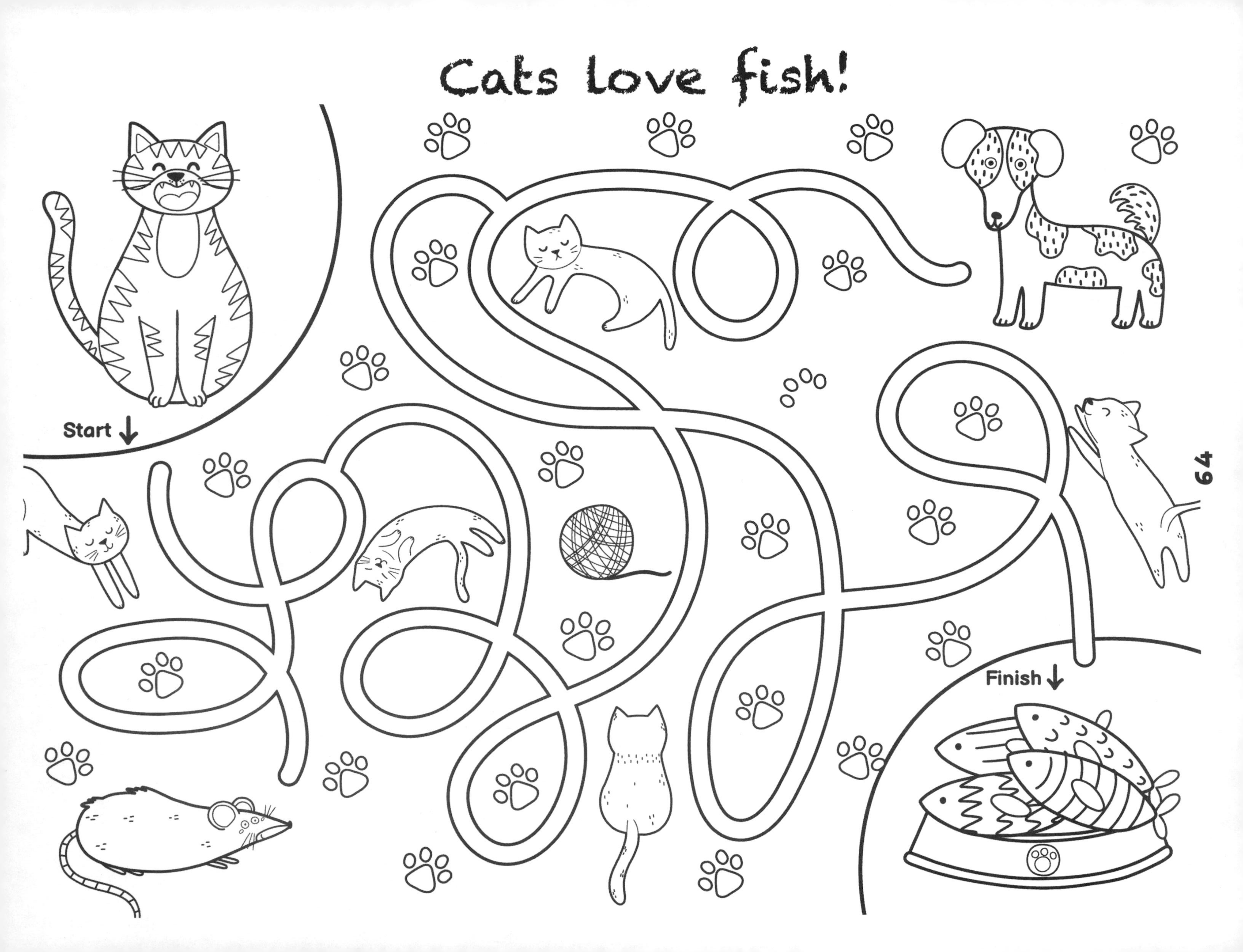
Cats love fish!
Start
Finish

SHAPE MAZE

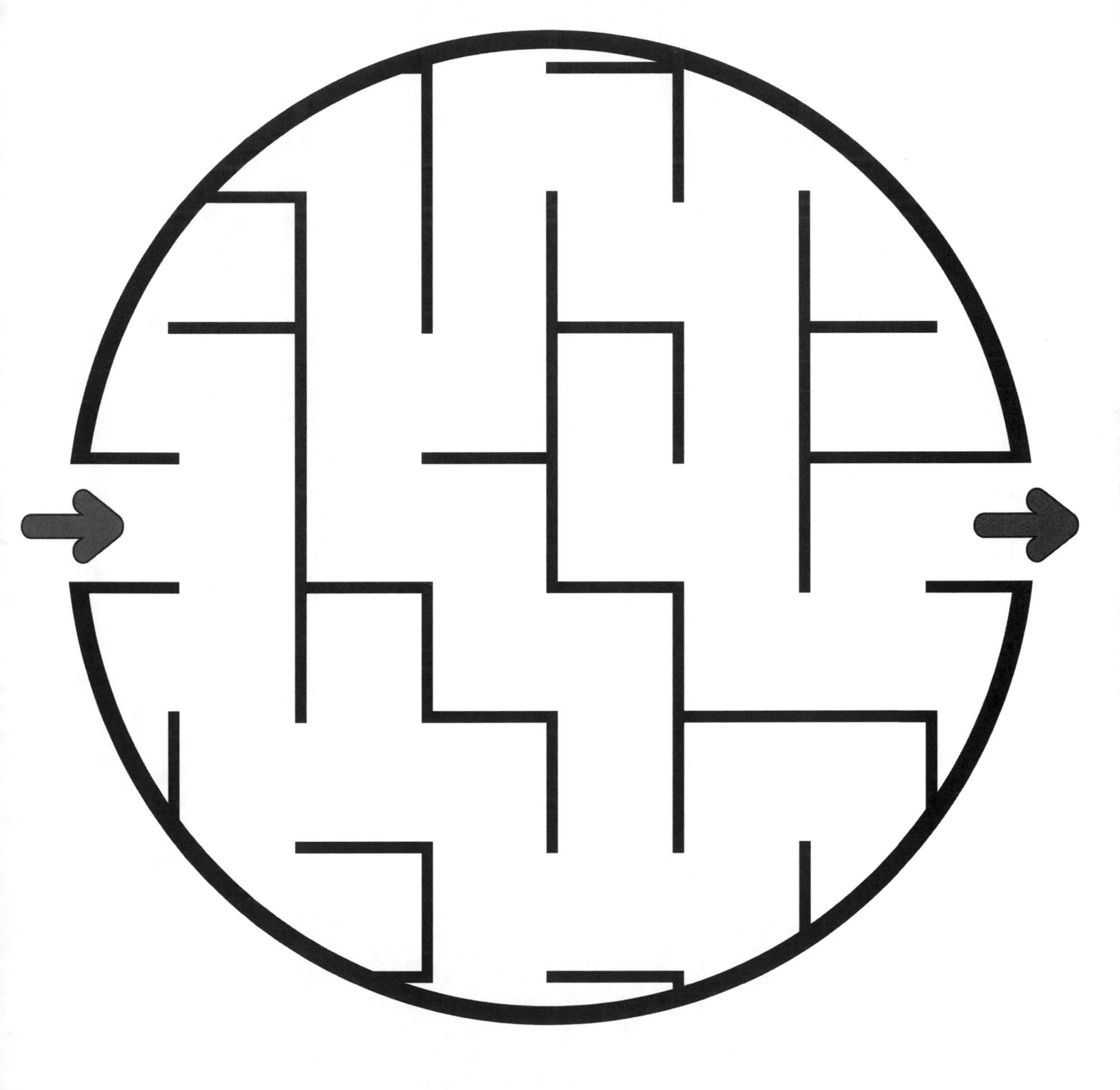

CIRCLE

I SEE YOU.
YOU SEE ME.

BOW TIE MAZE

Help the bee find
her flowers

JUMP ROPE

Get to the cheese. Safely!
Start
Finish

CORGI MAZE

Help Little Piggy Find Mommy

HELICOPTER

MAZE GAME
help the piglets to find the barn

KITTY MAZE

HELP THE SHIP GET TO EARTH!

MULTI-MAZE GAME

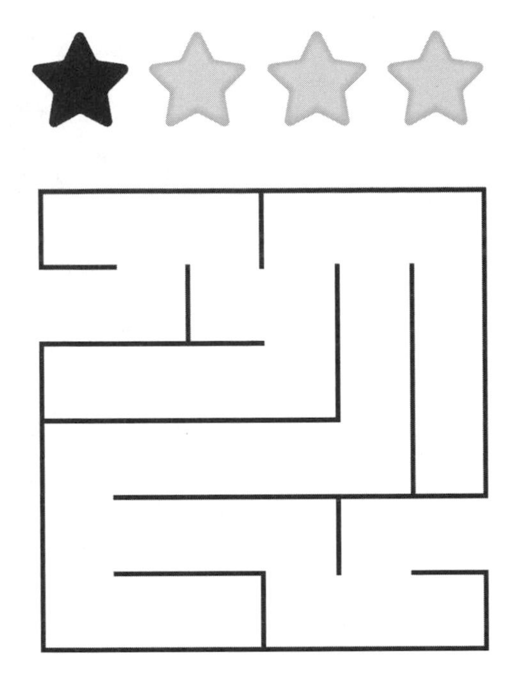

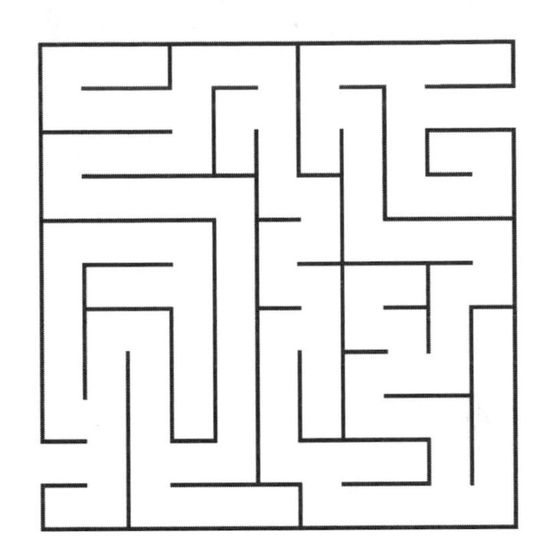

SPACE
Help the rocket to land on the Earth!

WHO WINS?

SWEET MAZE

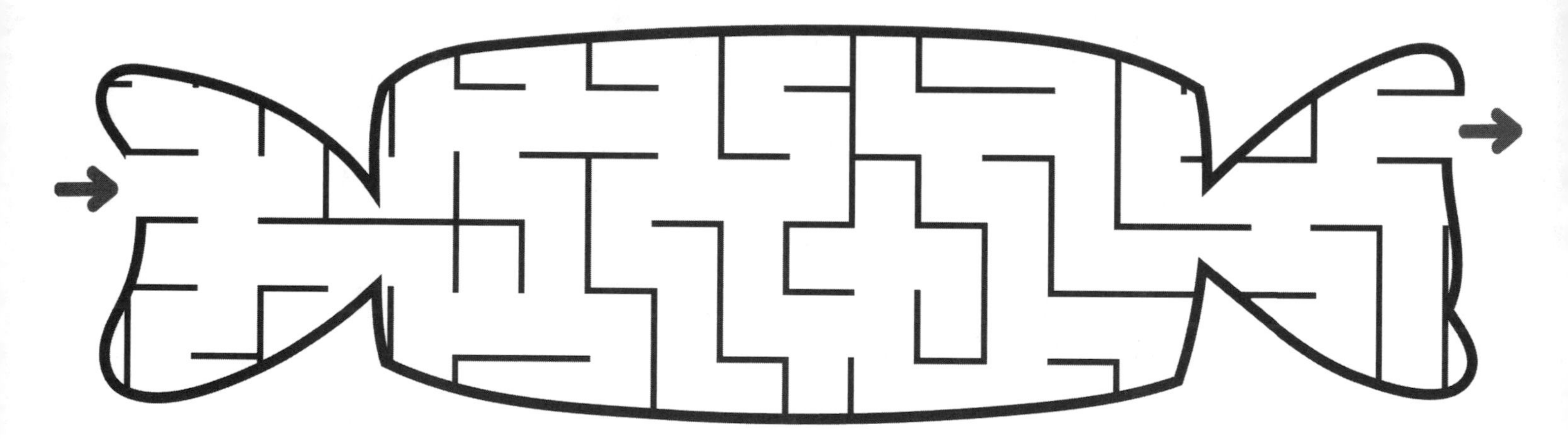

KICK THE BALL

HELP THE BUTTERFLY TO FIND THE YELLOW FLOWERS

WHO WINS?

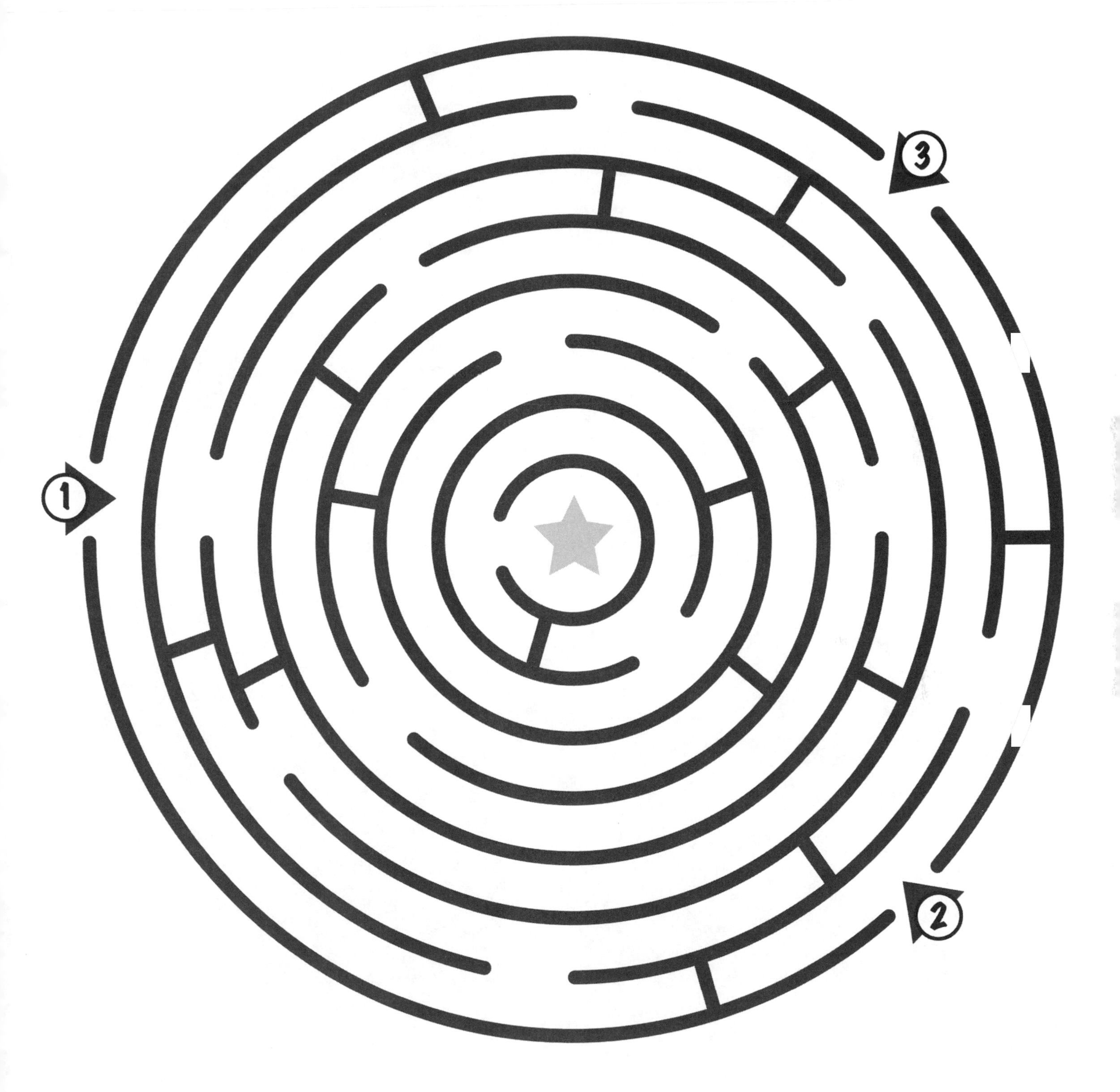

FOX EATS CHICKEN

GIRAFFE MAZE

Maze Game

design your own maze game.

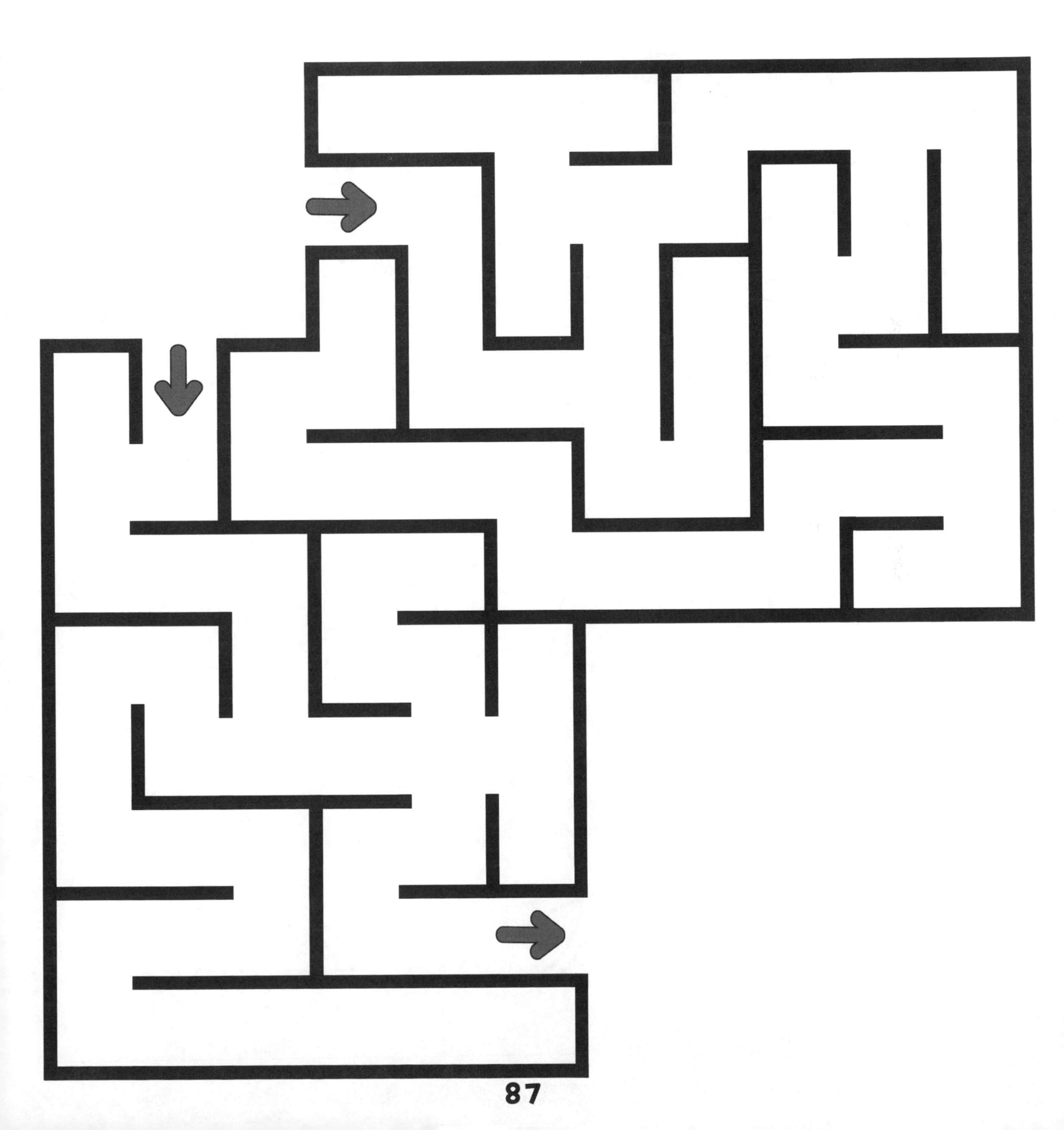

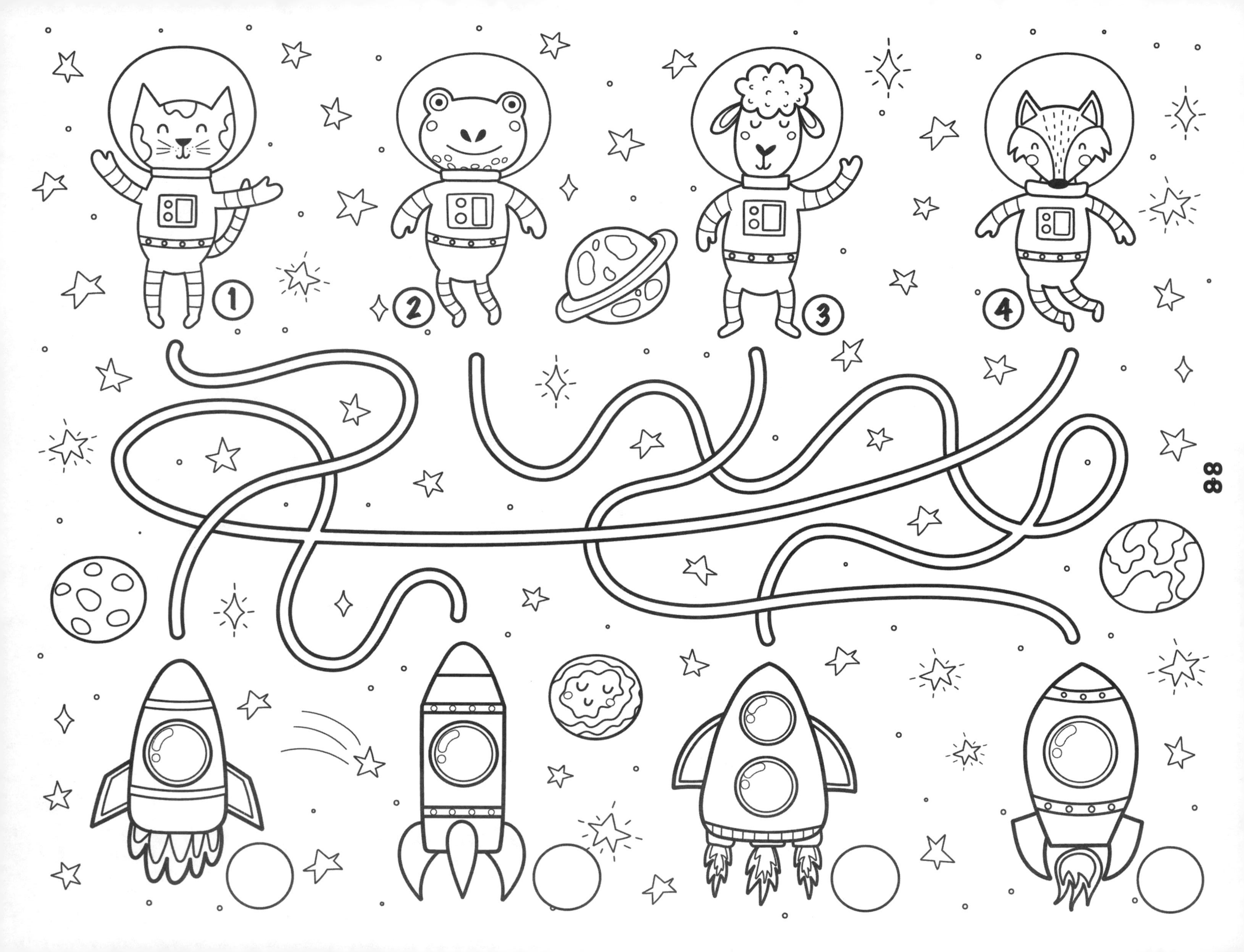
1
2
3
4

SHOOTING STAR

Find the squirrels nuts.
Start
Finish

SHAPE MAZE

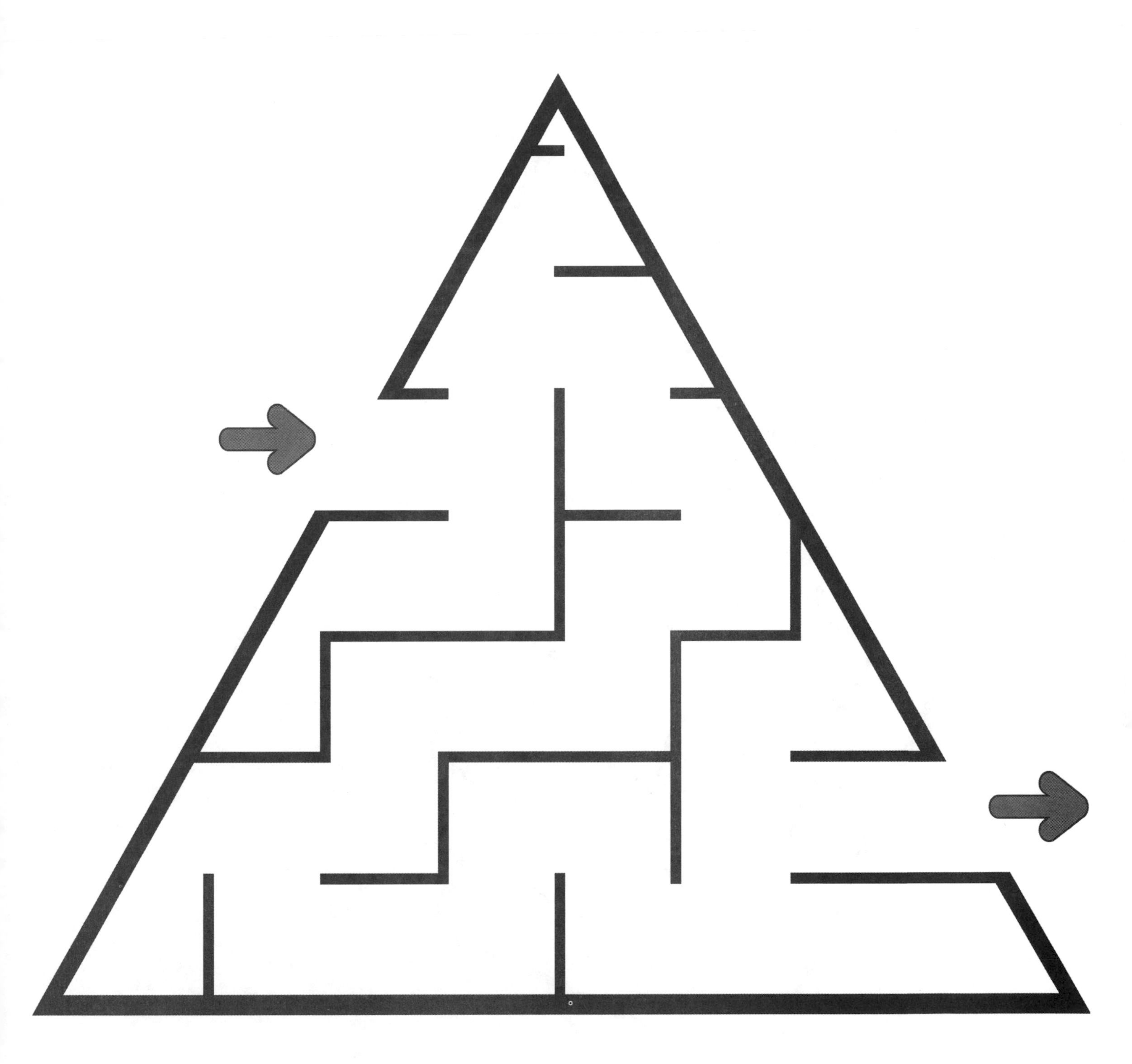

TRIANGLE

TREAT THE DOG

WHO WINS?

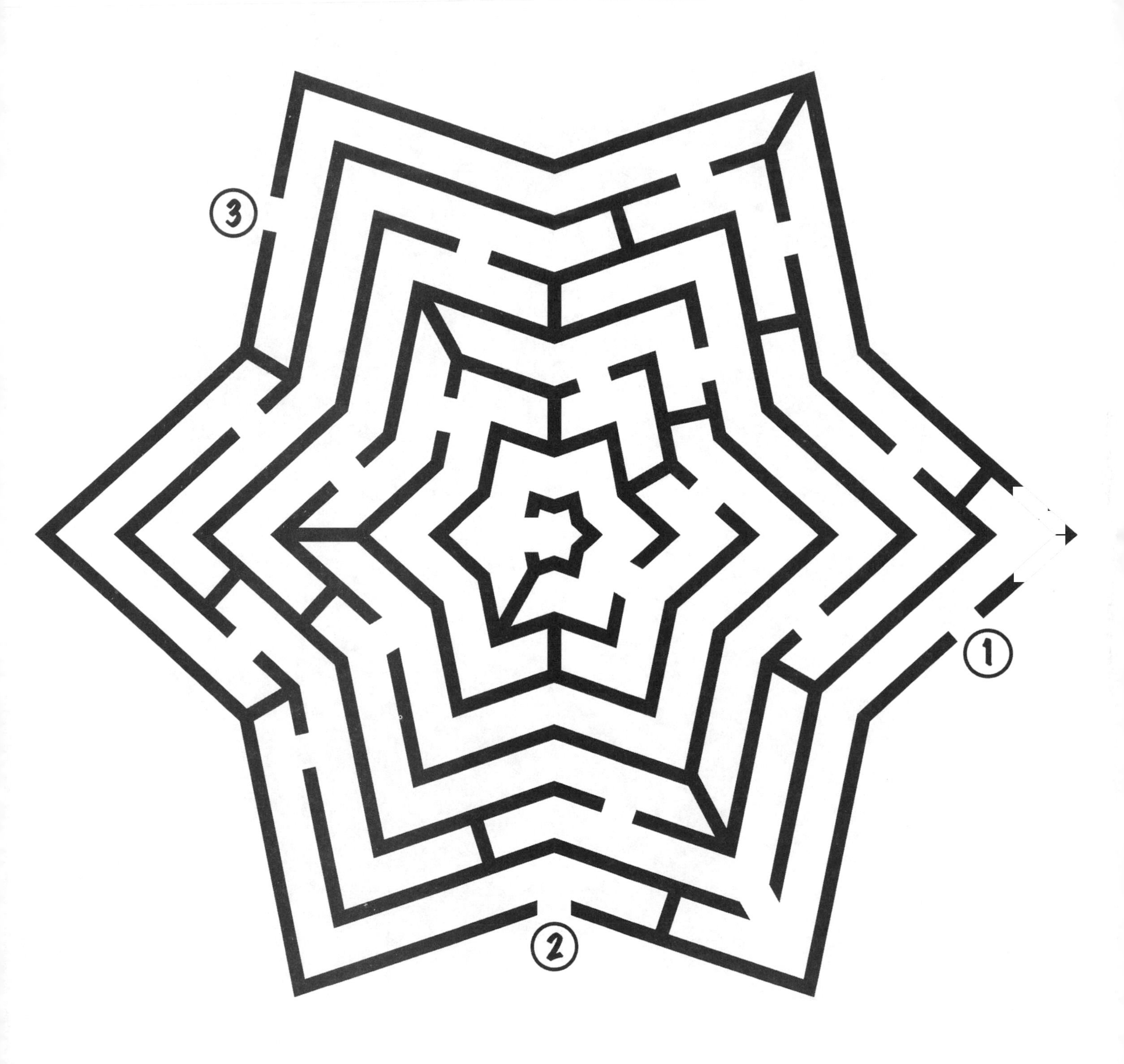

HELP THE ROCKET REACH THE PLANET

HELP
the MOUSE
to find
CHEESE
YOU
DONE!

CARRIAGE MAZE

Bees need flowers! Flowers need bees!

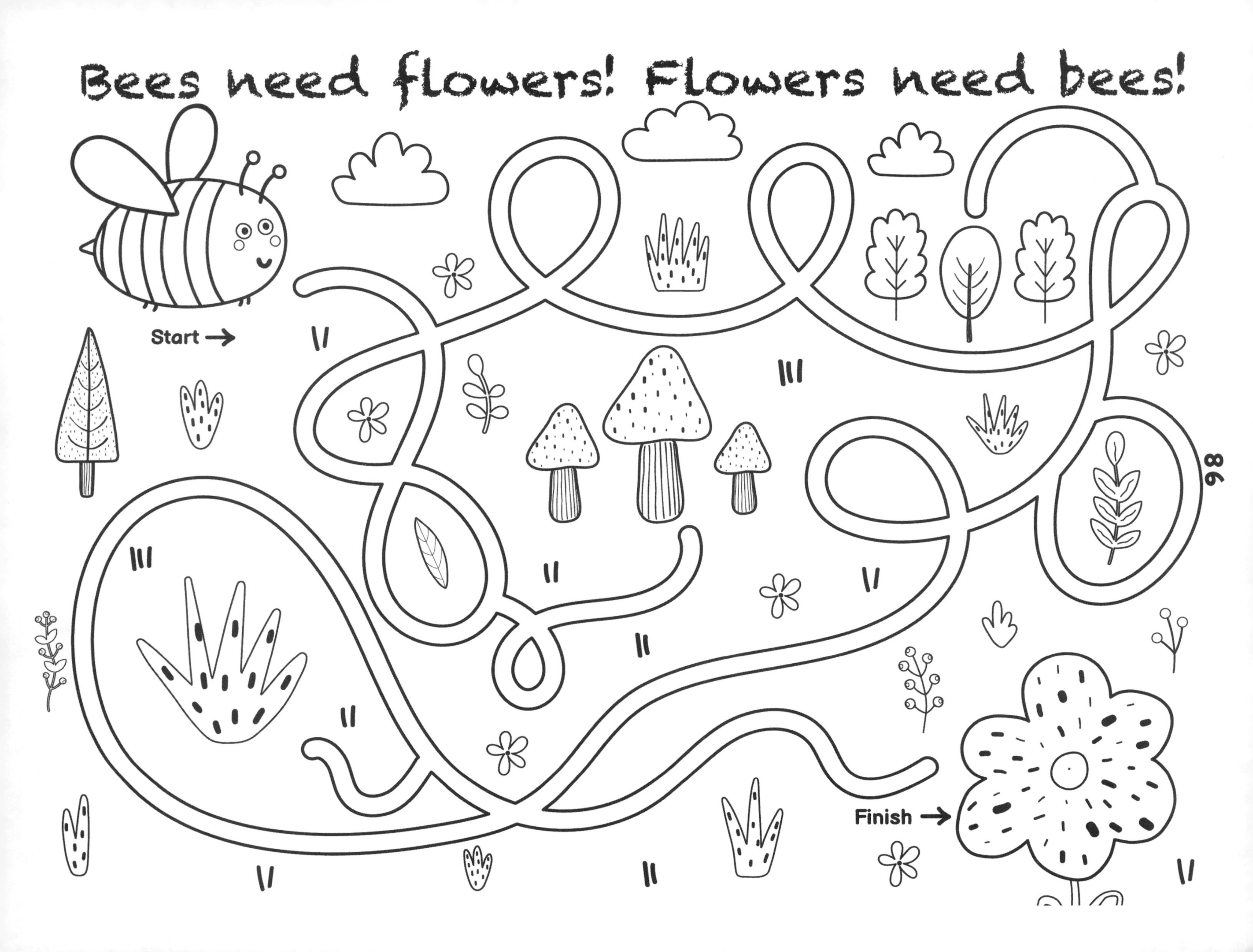

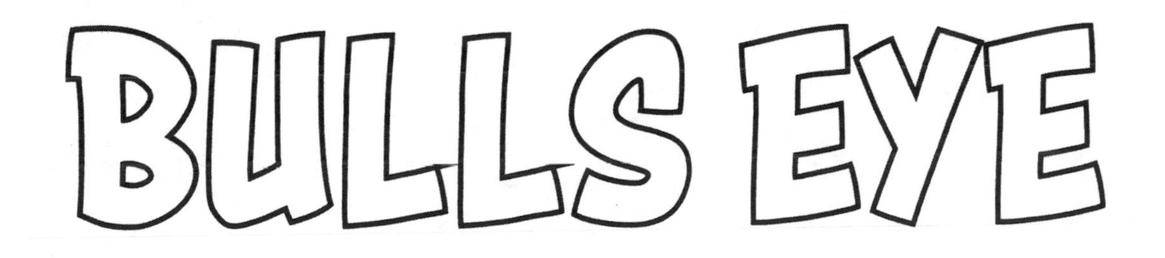
BULLS EYE

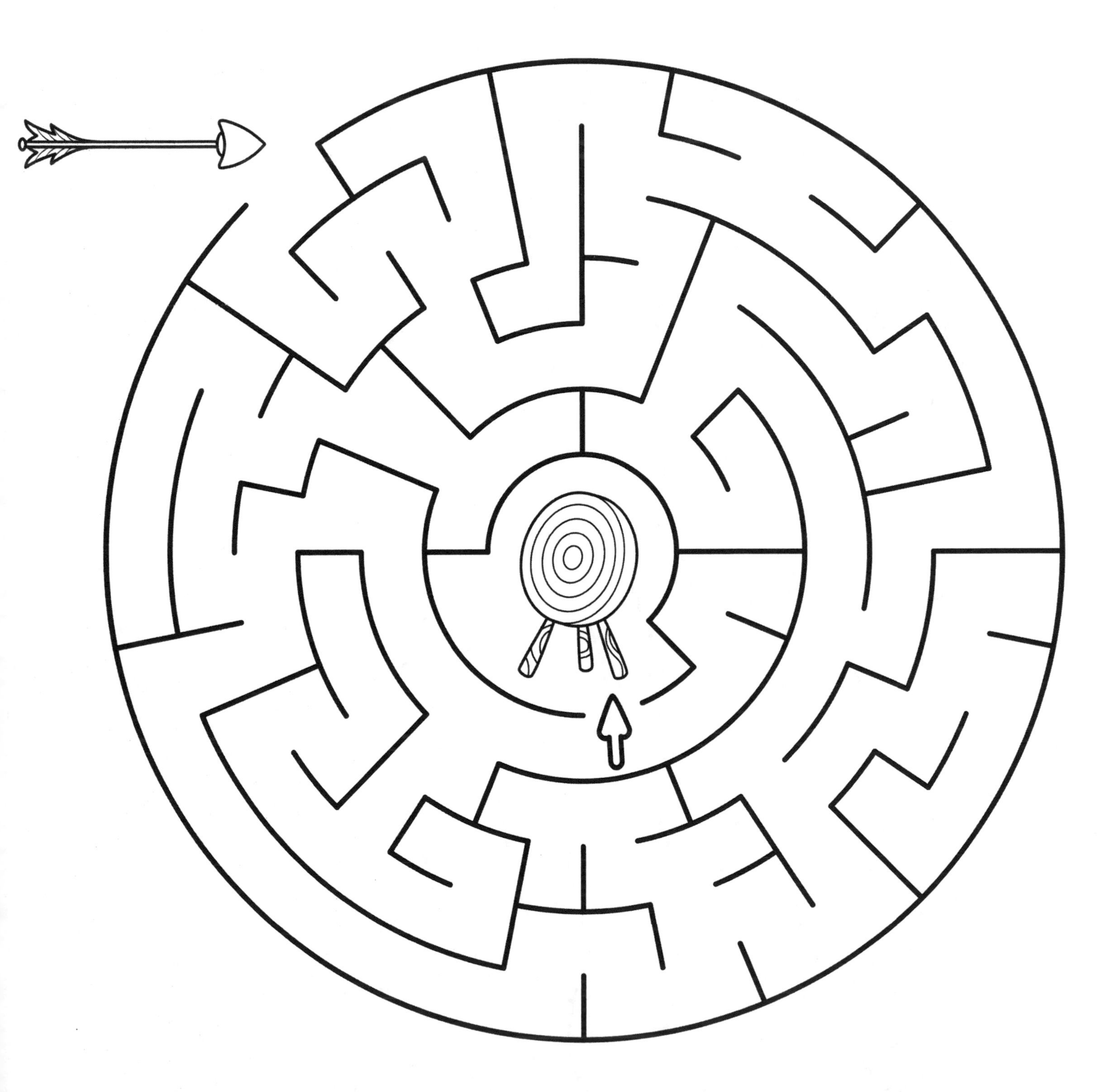

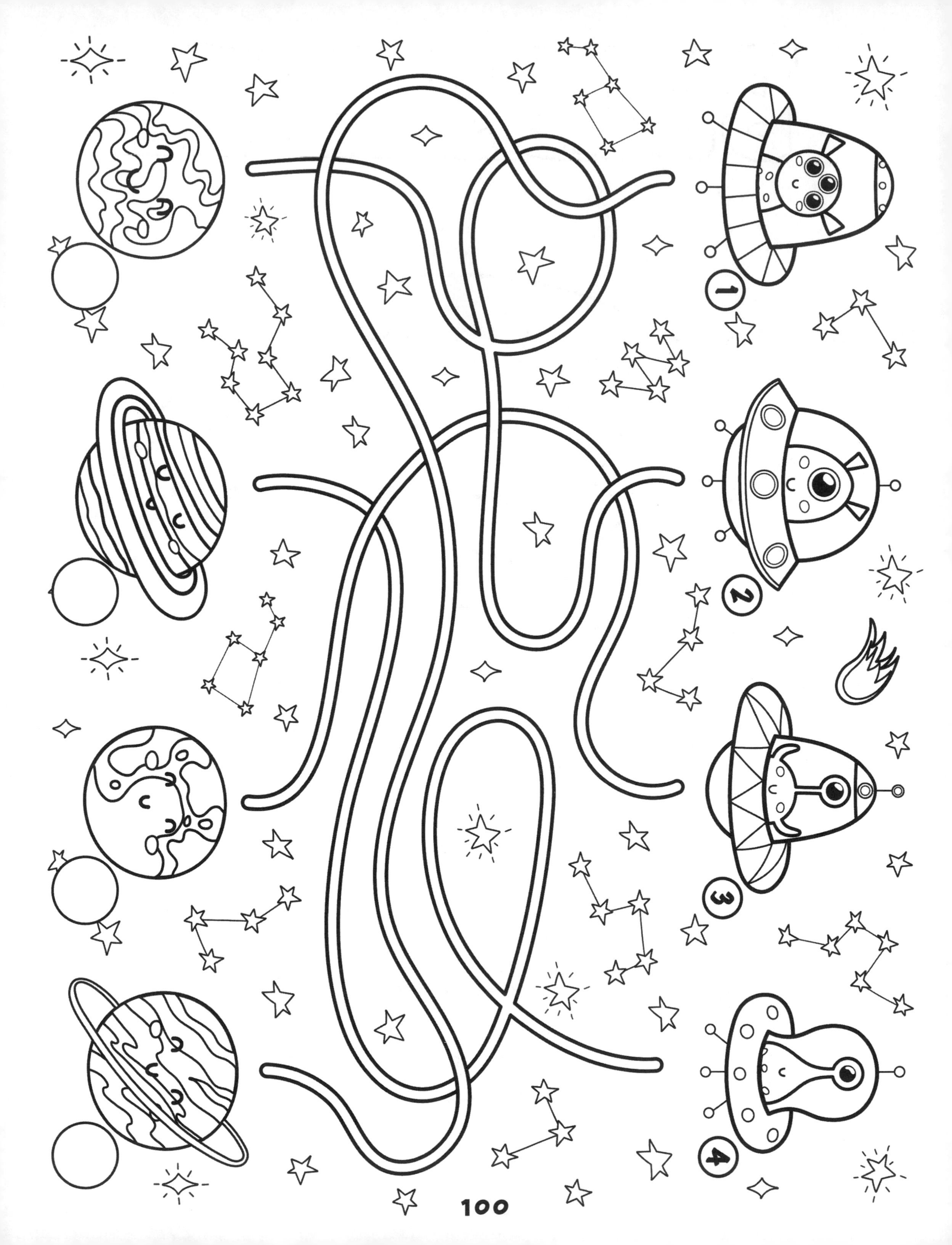
1
2
3
4

SEAHORSE

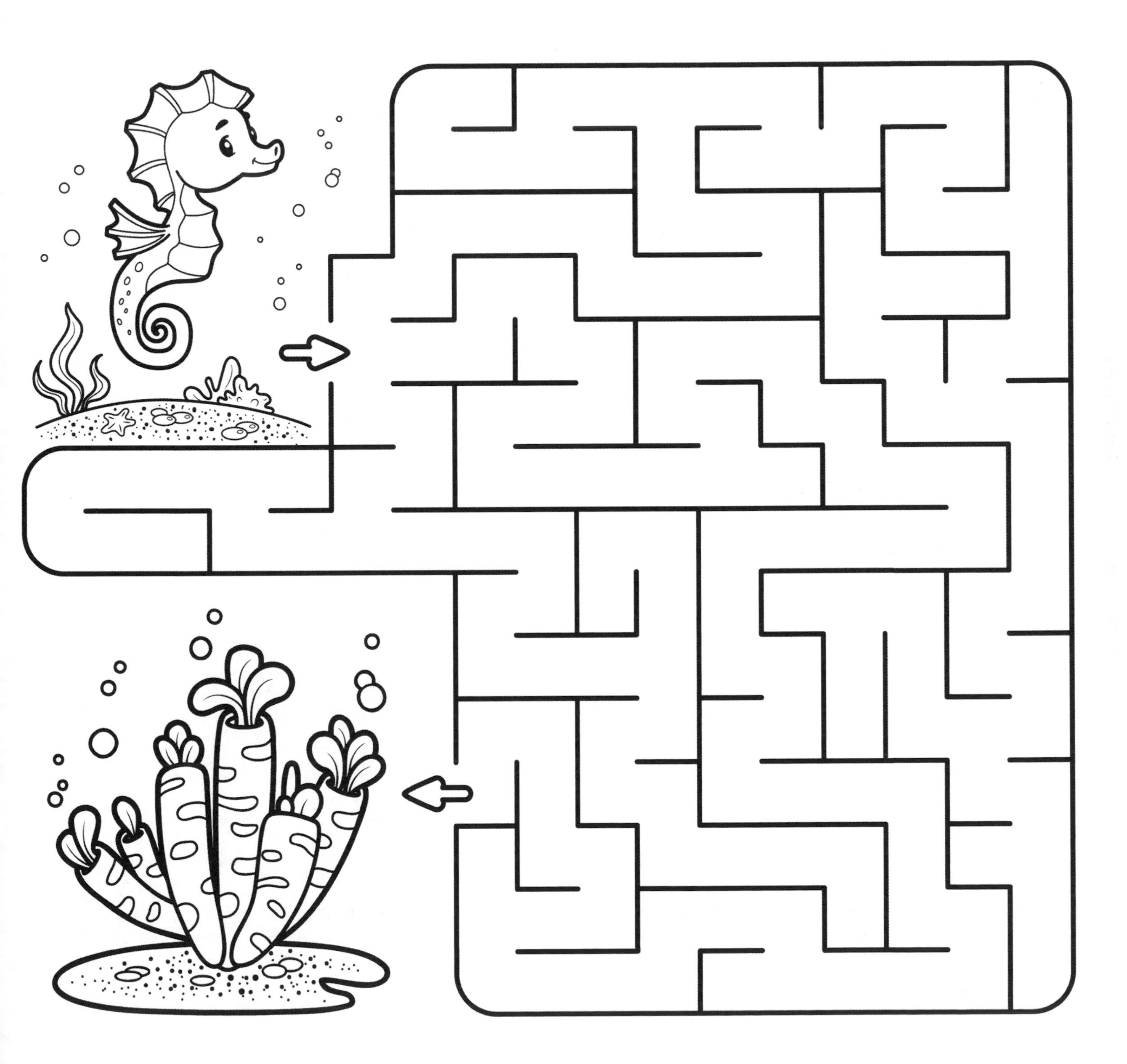

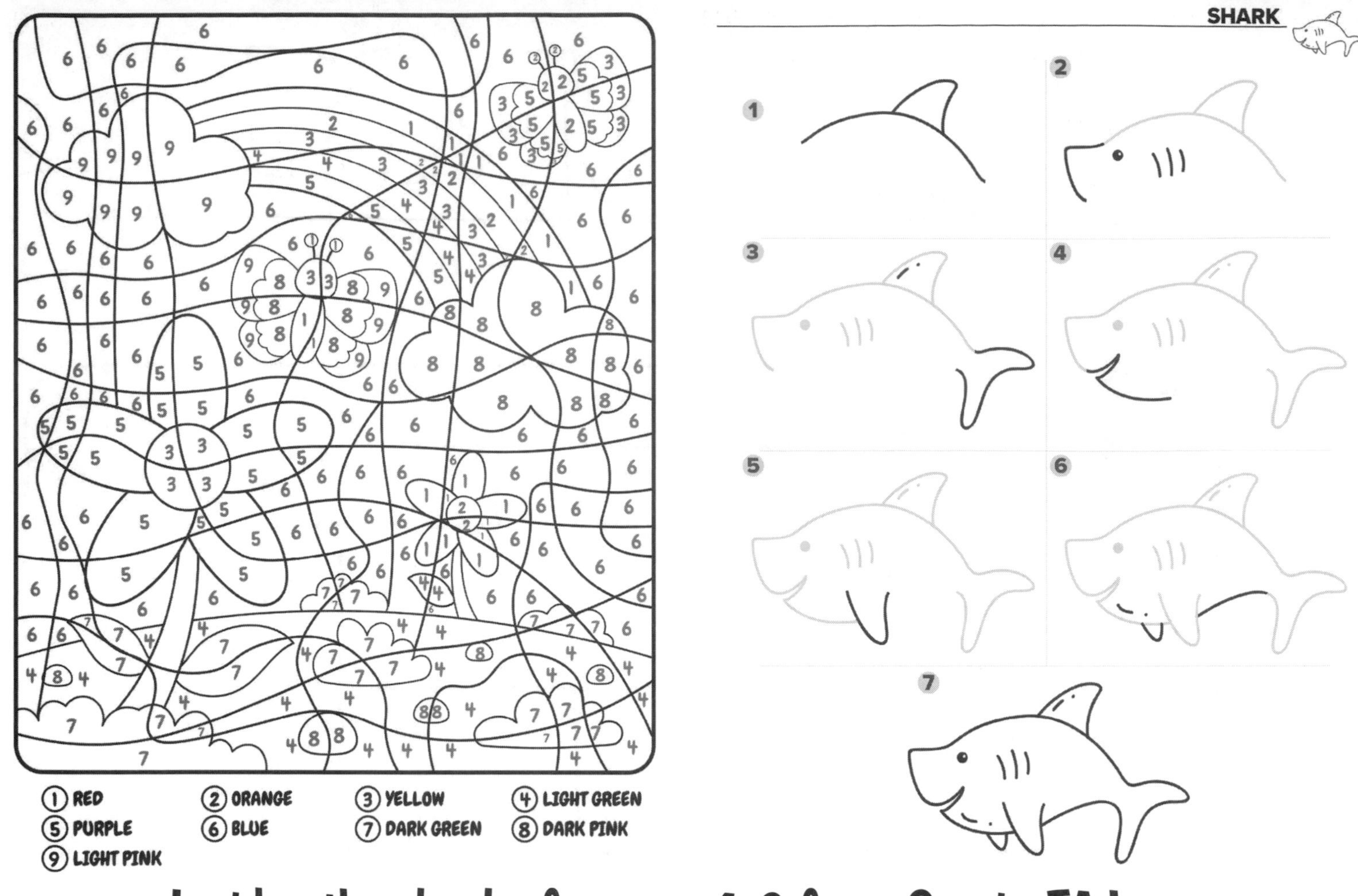

Inside other books for ages 4-8 from SamiraTAJ.com

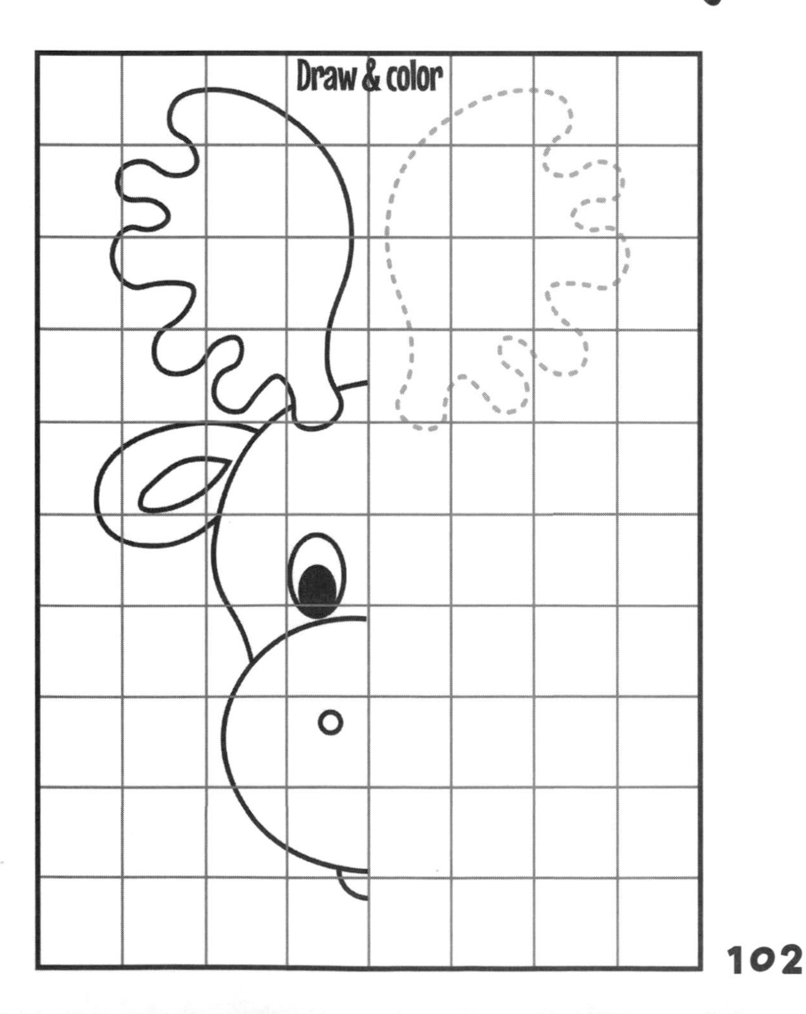

SUBMARINE 4
SNAIL MAZE 5
6
Quick! Get to the hospital.
DEER MAZE 7
WHOS LETTER HAS WHA 8
MULTI-MAZE GAM 9
WHO'S PRESENT 10
CUPID MAZE 11
12
What does SNAIL eat?
WHO WINS? 13
WHO'S BALLOON 14
SHAPE MAZE 15
SQUARE
16
Bath Time!
DOVE MAZE 17
18
Find Honey Maze
GORILLA MAZ 19

20
Here kitty, kitty...
WHO WINS?
21
LOST PUPPY MAZ
22
GET TO THE MIDD
23
24
Help Mommy T-Rex find her babies.
Start
Finish
SEAL MAZE
25
WOLF MAZE
26
SEAHORSE
27
28
Here puppy, puppy . . .
HELP SANTA
29
GET YOUR GIFT
HELP BABY PENGU
FIND THE IGLO
30
RACE TO THE MIDD
31
FLYING HEART
32
WHO WINS?
33
CAKE MAZE
34
35
Help the bunny
find sweets

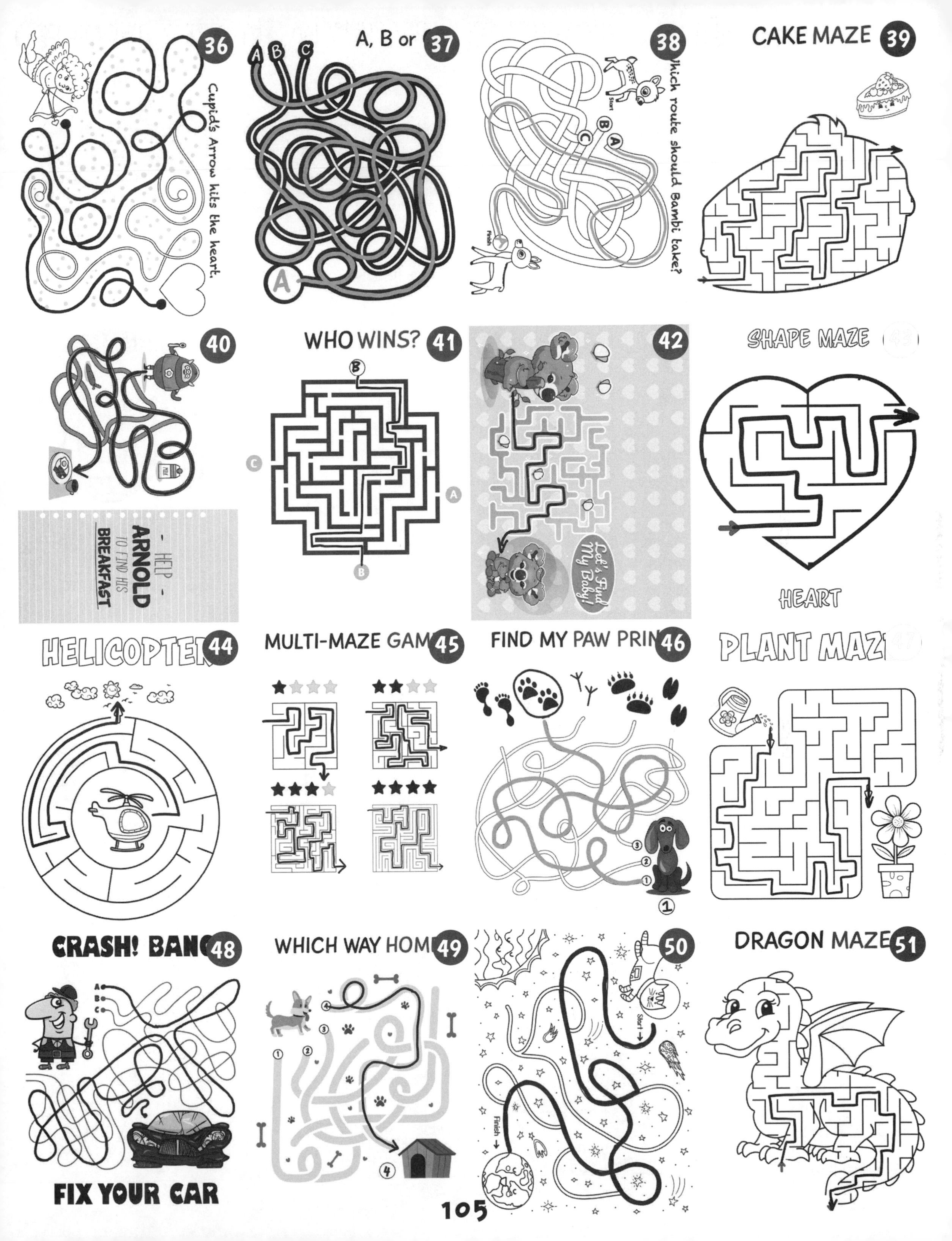
36
Cupid's Arrow hits the heart.
A, B or 37
A
B
C
A
38
Which route should Bambi take?
Start
Finish
A
B
C
CAKE MAZE 39
40
- HELP -
ARNOLD
TO FIND HIS
BREAKFAST
WHO WINS? 41
A
B
C
42
Let's Find My Baby!
SHAPE MAZE
HEART
HELICOPTER 44
MULTI-MAZE GAM 45
FIND MY PAW PRIN 46
1
2
3
PLANT MAZ
CRASH! BANG 48
A
B
C
FIX YOUR CAR
WHICH WAY HOM 49
1
2
3
4
50
Start
Finish
DRAGON MAZE 51

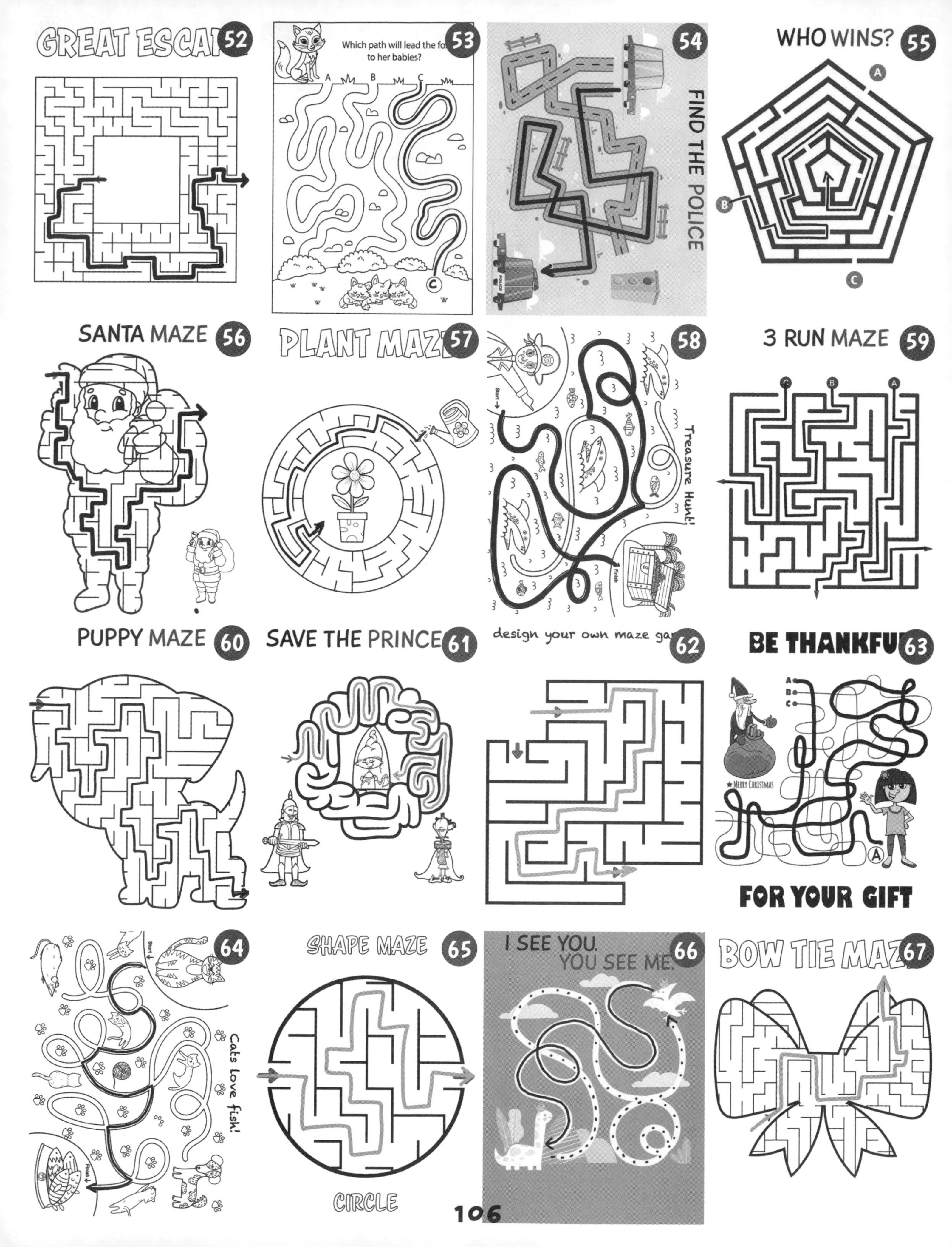
GREAT ESCAP
52
Which path will lead the fo
to her babies?
53
A
B
C
54
FIND THE POLICE
WHO WINS?
55
A
B
C
SANTA MAZE
56
PLANT MAZ
57
58
Treasure Hunt!
3 RUN MAZE
59
C
B
A
PUPPY MAZE
60
SAVE THE PRINCE
61
design your own maze ga
62
BE THANKFU
63
A
B
C
MERRY CHRISTMAS
FOR YOUR GIFT
64
Cats love fish!
SHAPE MAZE
65
CIRCLE
I SEE YOU.
YOU SEE ME.
66
BOW TIE MAZ
67

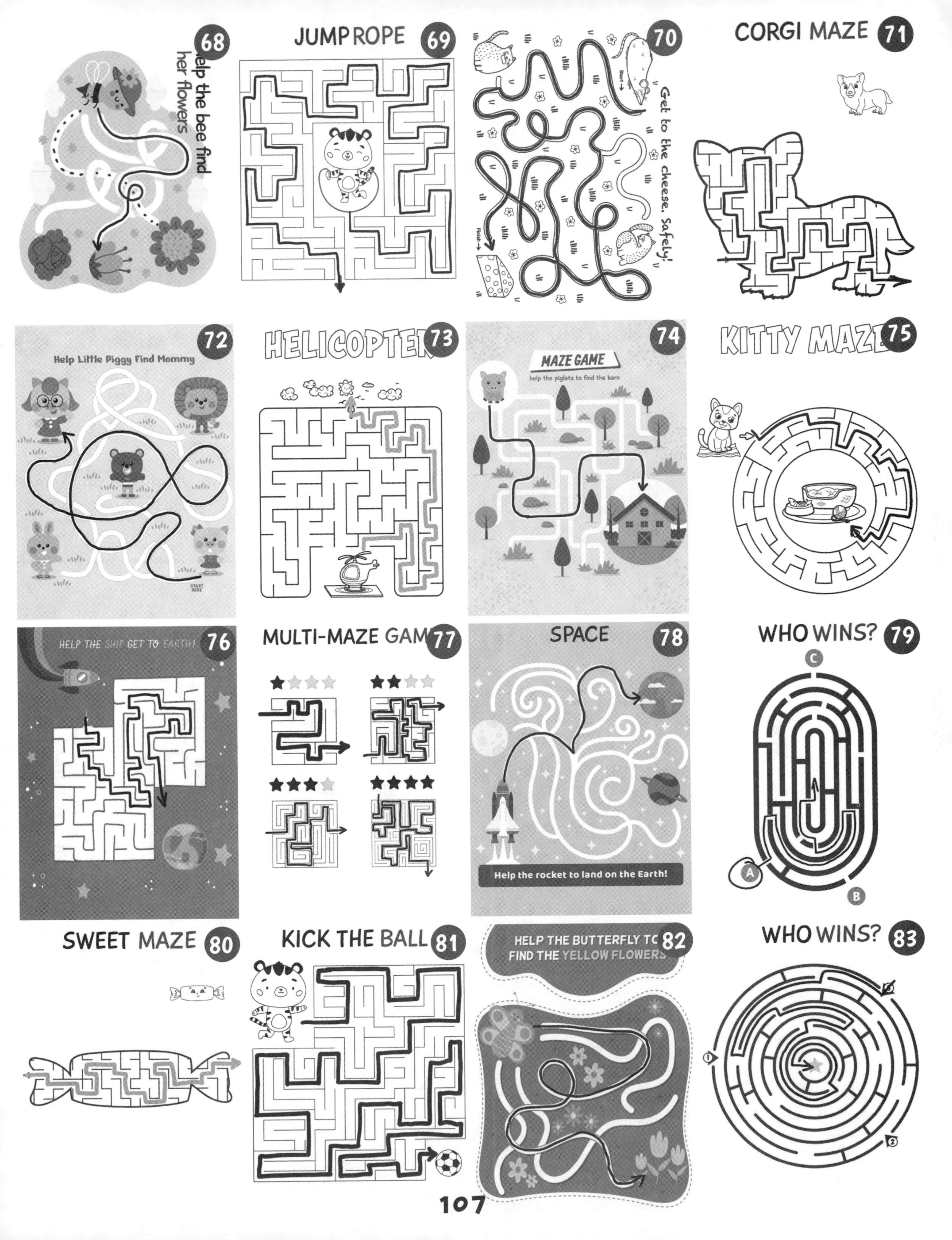
68
Help the bee find her flowers
JUMP ROPE
69
70
Get to the cheese. Safely!
Start
Finish
CORGI MAZE
71
72
Help Little Piggy Find Mommy
START HERE
HELICOPTER
73
74
MAZE GAME
help the piglets to find the barn
KITTY MAZE
75
HELP THE SHIP GET TO EARTH!
76
MULTI-MAZE GAME
77
SPACE
78
Help the rocket to land on the Earth!
WHO WINS?
79
C
A
B
SWEET MAZE
80
KICK THE BALL
81
HELP THE BUTTERFLY TO FIND THE YELLOW FLOWERS
82
WHO WINS?
83
1
2

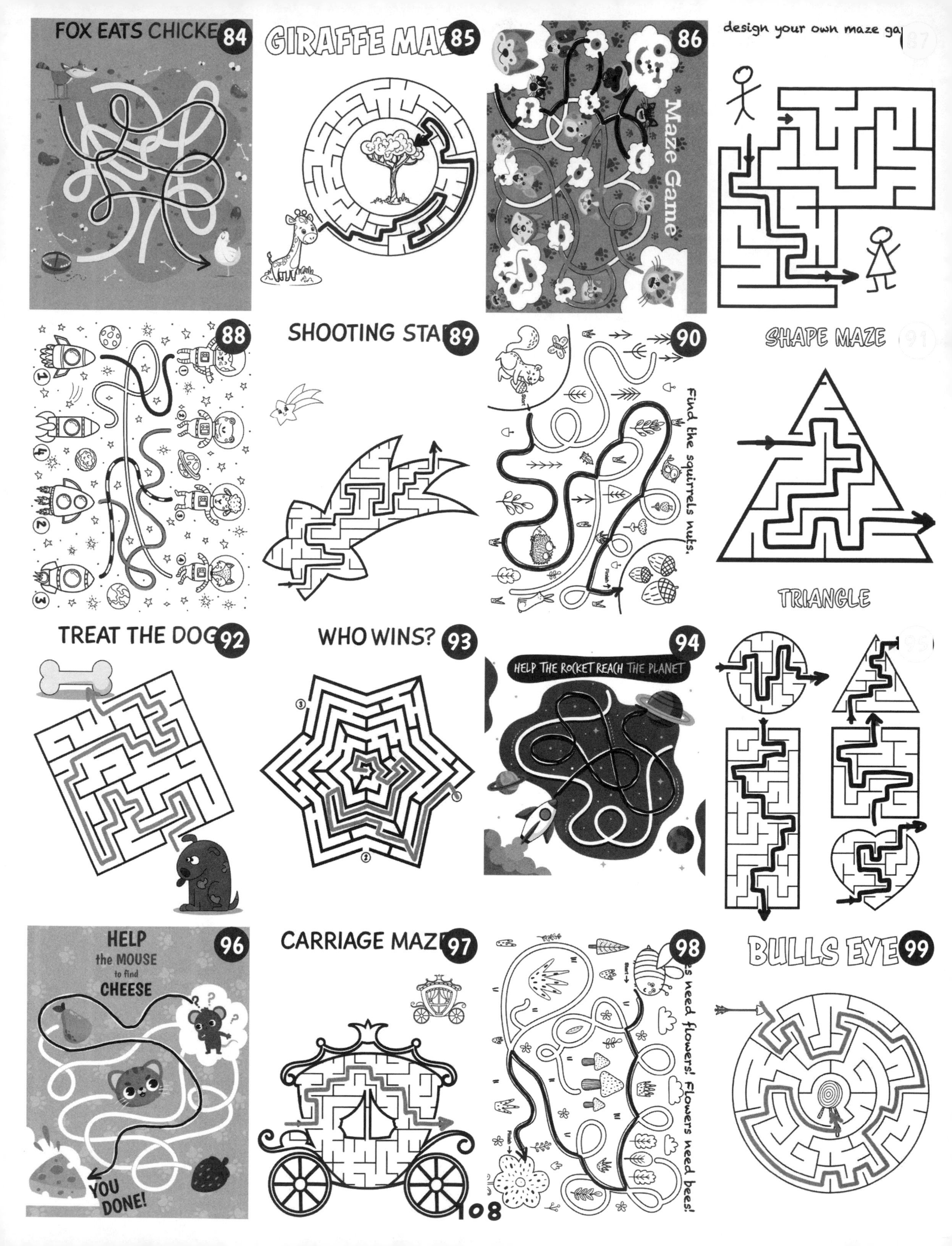
FOX EATS CHICKE
84
GIRAFFE MAZ
85
86
Maze Game
design your own maze ga
87
88
SHOOTING STA
89
90
Find the squirrels nuts.
SHAPE MAZE
91
TRIANGLE
TREAT THE DOG
92
WHO WINS?
93
94
HELP THE ROCKET REACH THE PLANET
95
HELP
the MOUSE
to find
CHEESE
YOU
DONE!
96
CARRIAGE MAZ
97
98
Bees need flowers! Flowers need bees!
BULLS EYE
99

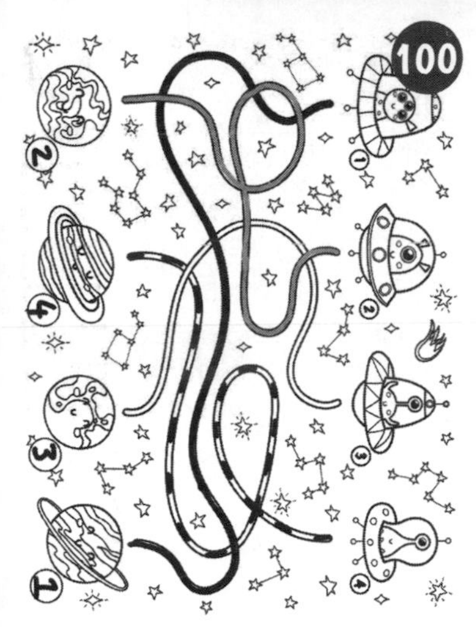

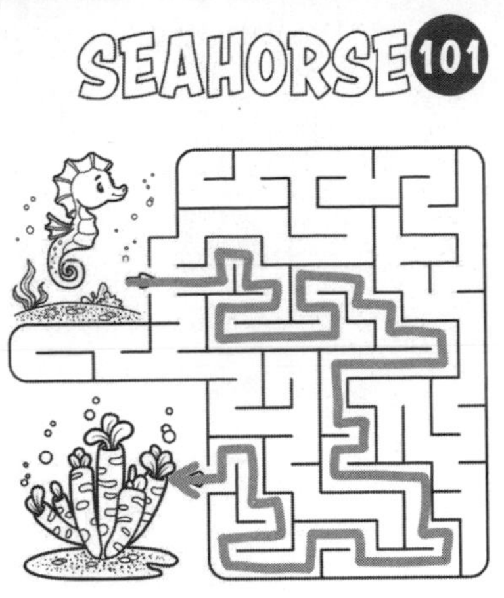

samirataj.com

Please consider leaving an honest review to let us know how your Little Genius found our Puzzle book.

This helps other buyers make informed decisions.

SAMIRA
ages 4-8
CONGRATULATIONS
MAZES
CERTIFICATE
OF COMPLETION
AWARDED TO :
AGE :
DATE :
DOWNLOAD YOUR
COLOR CERTIFICATE
AT SamiraTAJ.COM
fun
To
THE
MOON

MORE BOOKS

SamiraTAJ has many full color vibrantly illustrated activity books, well thought out puzzle books, and coloring books for your Little Genius.

Designed to help little ones practice and improve their fine motor skills, auditory attention, and concentration. Working through the books together will boost your child's academic confidence.

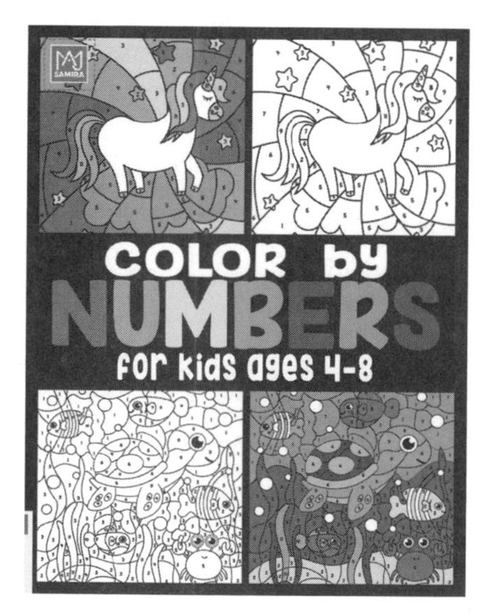

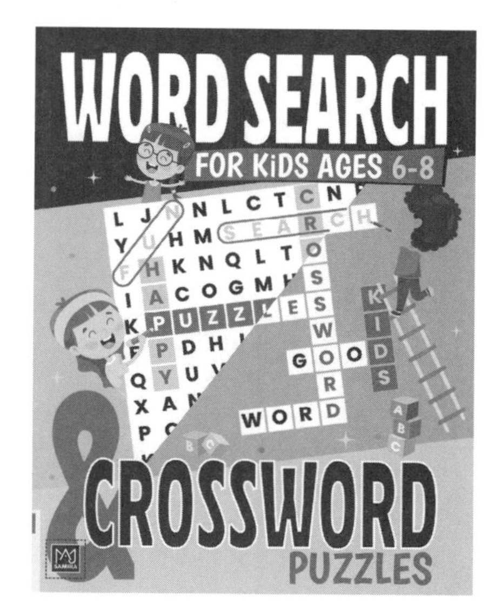

samirataj.com